THE SWEET SPOT

A KROYDON HILLS LEGACY NOVEL

PLAYING TO WIN
BOOK FOUR

BELLA MATTHEWS

Copyright © 2024

Bella Matthews

All rights reserved. No part of this publication may be reproduced or transmitted by any means, electronic, mechanical, photocopying, recording or otherwise, without the prior permission of the publisher, except in the case of brief quotation embodied in the critical reviews and certain other noncommercial uses permitted by copyright law.

Without in any way limiting the author's exclusive rights under copyright, any use of this publication to "train" generative artificial intelligence (AI) technologies to generate text is expressly prohibited. The author reserves all rights to license uses of this work for generative AI training and development of machine learning language models.

This is a work of fiction, created without use of AI technology. Resemblance to actual persons, things, living or dead, locales or events is entirely coincidental. The author acknowledges the trademark status and trademark owners of various products referenced in this work of fiction, which have been used without permission. The publication/use of these trademarks is not authorized, associated with, or sponsored by the trademark owners.

This book contains mature themes and is only suitable for 18+ readers.

Editor: Dena Mastrogiovanni, Red Pen Editing

Proofreader: Emma Cook | Booktastic Blonde LLC

Cover Designer: Sarah Sentz, Enchanting Romance Designs

Photographer: Michelle Lancaster

Interior Formatting: Brianna Cooper

SENSITIVE CONTENT

This book contains sensitive content that could be triggering.
Please see my website for a full list.

WWW.AUTHORBELLAMATTHEWS.COM

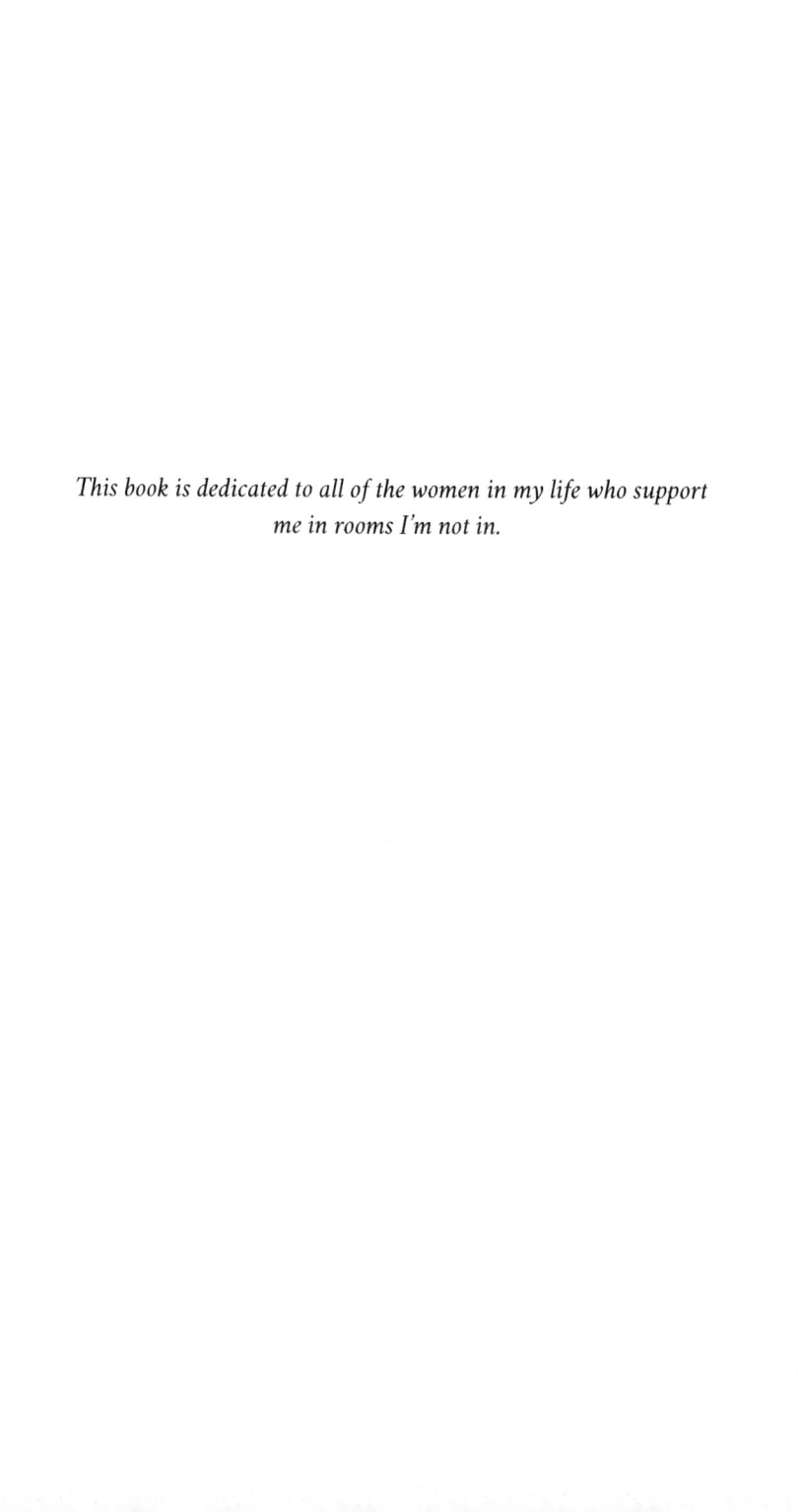

This book is dedicated to all of the women in my life who support me in rooms I'm not in.

She's the kind of queen that knows her crown isn't on her head but in her soul.

— ADRIAN MICHAEL

CAST OF CHARACTERS

The Kings Of Kroydon Hills Family

- **Declan & Annabelle Sinclair**
    - Everly Sinclair - 24
    - Grace Sinclair - 24
    - Nixon Sinclair - 23
    - Leo Sinclair - 22
    - Hendrix Sinclair - 19

- **Brady & Nattie Ryan**
    - Noah Ryan - 21
    - Lilah Ryan - 21
    - Dillan Ryan - 18
    - Asher Ryan - 12

- **Aiden & Sabrina Murphy**
    - Jameson Murphy -21
    - Finn Murphy - 18

- **Bash & Lenny Beneventi**
    - Maverick Beneventi - 21
    - Ryker Beneventi - 19

- **Cooper & Carys Sinclair**
    - Lincoln Sinclair - 14
    - Lochlan Sinclair - 14
    - Lexie Sinclair - 14

- **Coach Joe & Catherine Sinclair**
    - Callen Sinclair - 24

The Kingston Family

- **Ashlyn & Brandon Dixon**
    - Madeline Kingston - 25
    - Raven Dixon - 9

- **Max & Daphne Kingston**
    - Serena Kingston - 18

- **Scarlet & Cade St. James**
    - Brynlee St. James - 24
    - Killian St. James - 22
    - Olivia St. James - 20

- **Becket & Juliette Kingston**
    - Easton Hayes - 29
    - Kenzie Hayes - 23
    - Blaise Kingston - 13

- **Sawyer & Wren Kingston**
    - Knox Kingston - 17
    - Crew Kingston - 14

- **Hudson & Maddie Kingston**
    - Teagan Kingston - 18
    - Aurora Kingston - 15
    - Brooklyn Kingston - 10

- **Amelia & Sam Beneventi**
    - Maddox Beneventi - 23
    - Caitlin Beneventi - 20
    - Roman Beneventi - 18

    ○ Lucky Beneventi - 16

- **Lenny & Bash Beneventi**
    ○ Maverick Beneventi - 21
    ○ Ryker Beneventi - 19

- **Jace & India Kingston**
    ○ Cohen Kingston - 17
    ○ Saylor Kingston - 12
    ○ Atlas Kingston - 9
    ○ Asher Kingston - 9

>   For family trees, please visit my website
>   www.authorbellamatthews.com

BRYNLEE

The stale scent of spilled beer mingles with the sweet smell of sunscreen on the insane number of bodies crowding in around me, while I try not to get smashed up against my favorite beach bar. *Literally.* The place is packed tonight, and based on the sheer wave of bodies moving in sync to the beat of the music, I'm fairly sure everyone in the entire town is crammed in here, singing along to "Sweet Caroline."

It's summertime at O'Malley's, and I wouldn't change a thing.

This place has been around since my parents were kids, and according to them, it's always been this crazy. It's one of those bars you know better than to wear nice shoes in because you know you're leaving at the end of the night with questionable substances on them. Spilled beer being the least gross of those substances. And I'm pretty sure the bartender is still the same one who was working here ten years ago when my cousin Maddox and I came in with our very first fake ID's.

A quick elbow to the back has me stumbling as Maddox hands me a margarita and passes out the rest of the drinks to our friends and family before we all raise our glasses. "*Alla faccia di chi ci vuole.*"

"In English, please," his younger sister, Caitlin, snaps at him as a round of *Salute* is uttered back by everyone else before we all clink our glasses together and drink.

I swallow a mouthful of tequila with a hint of lime and choke as my mouth catches fire. "Oh wow." The words burn almost as much as the tequila as it makes its way down my throat. "That's bad."

Callen slings his big, beefy arm around my shoulders and guides me to a now-empty bar stool. "Drink it faster, Brynlee. You won't taste it as much."

I hop up and spin my stool to face Maddox and him.

Even sitting on a barstool, these two tower over me.

Everyone does.

Short girl problems.

"You realize that defeats the purpose, right? I don't drink something if I don't like the taste." I stir the concoction that should never be anyone's definition of a margarita, hoping that will help before taking another sip. *Nope.* Still bad.

Maddox ignores me and hands Callen and me each shot glasses as the rest of our friends disburse to other parts of the bar.

I sniff the dark liquid and scrunch my nose, not in the mood to get burned twice. "What is this?"

"Don't ask." Maddox lifts his shot glass up much the same way we did a minute ago, and the three of us clink glasses again before Callen sets his sights on a bachelorette party at the end of the bar like a heat seeking missile.

"I think I'm gonna go bag me a bride."

Maddox looks down the bar and shakes his head. "Jesus

Christ, Callen. You're gonna get yourself killed one of these days."

"Nah, man." Callen just keeps smiling as he claps Maddox on the shoulder. "You won't let me die."

Callen disappears down the bar into a circle of bridesmaids, and I stifle a laugh. "Think we'll see him again tonight?"

"Doubt it," Maddox scoffs.

I push my margarita toward the bartender with my sweetest smile. "Hey, Lou. Think you could add more mix to this?"

Lou looks down my shirt before making eye contact. "Most people usually ask for more booze."

"Most people who want to live wouldn't look at her tits either, man. So how about you just do it, huh?" Maddox's beer hits the bar a little harder than necessary as he glares at the old man. Guess you could say my cousin is a touch overprotective.

Lou's eyes double in size before he quickly takes my glass away to fix my drink.

Hopefully, the next one won't incinerate my taste buds.

"Did you have to scare him?" I nail Maddox with my attempt at a glare, already tired and wondering how long I have to stay here before I can go back to the house and crash in my warm, comfy bed.

Maddox cocks his head like an apex predator, silently answering me.

Like I didn't already know the damn answer.

Everyone in this town knows exactly who Maddox Beneventi is. Or more accurately, who his father, Sam, is. And as my uncle likes to say, *a little bit* of fear is healthy. I glance at the bartender, who's currently pouring my new drink with shaking hands. This dude has passed *a little bit* and is well on his way to terrified.

Madman, as those of us who aren't scared love to call him, shrugs before he leans back against the bar. With crossed arms, his tight black t-shirt looks like it's defying the laws of something . . . *physics maybe*, as it stretches across his chest. He looks around, taking the space in. Probably checking for his sister, making sure she's not causing any trouble. Knowing Caitlin, she's already relocated to the beach area at the back of the bar, as far away from her big brother and his prying eyes as possible. *Smart girl.*

Lou pushes my drink across the bar with a still-shaking hand before heading to the other end, and I give up on any attempt not to laugh. "You know you're a dick, right?"

"Tell me something I don't know." Dark eyes look over the top of his beer at me, and he grins. "Although I'm pretty sure I'm the one with the information you might want tonight. So maybe it's me who needs to be doing the telling."

I stir my fresh margarita before taking a sip.

Ohh . . . So much better.

"What are you talking about?" I press, intrigued. "What do you know?"

"The better question is who do I know *about*," he taunts, clearly enjoying himself.

This fucker.

"What's it worth to you?" His lips pull up with mischief.

The song switches to a Bon Jovi classic, and the entire bar goes wild. A pretty girl in a denim miniskirt and a tiny little crop top stumbles into Maddox's chest, and I think he actually growls at her until she staggers away.

Hmm . . . it's not like him to ignore a pretty girl. I'll have to remember to press him on that *after* I find out what the hell he's hiding. "Come on, Madman. Spill it."

I sip my drink slowly and enjoy the smooth way it goes down.

I love tequila. It doesn't usually love me back. But so is life.

"Again, what's it worth to you?" The cocky fucker sits his beer on the bar and turns to face me head-on, smiling like an evil cherub. "And before you answer, think really hard."

I run my finger around the salt-rimmed glass, too tired to play this game. "Quit being so damn cryptic and tell me what you know."

He cocks an already cocky dark brow. "You're not going to like it."

"Since when has that ever stopped you before?" I challenge.

Maddox finishes his beer and points the empty bottle at Lou before bringing his eyes back to me. "Don't say I didn't warn you."

"So dramatic," I tease and wait for him to give up the goods.

Seriously . . . how bad can it be?

"Your Mom is gonna have you moved from working with the Revolution to the Kings team," he lays out before accepting his new beer while I sit staring in disbelief.

"But I'm the physical therapist for the Revolution . . ." I argue. "She can't just have me switched from the hockey team to the football team. They're different organizations altogether." But before I even finish the sentence, I know I'm wrong. Scarlet Kingston-St. James is the vice president of King Corp. She's the general manager of the Philadelphia Kings football team, and she works closely with my Uncle Max, her oldest brother, King Corp.'s president and the GM for the Revolution, which also makes him my boss. "Just because she could technically do that doesn't mean she would. Hate to break it to you—but looks like you're wrong."

"I'm not," is all the response I get. If he's trying to get under my skin, it's working.

"You are. There's no way my mom would do that to me. She's proud of my career. She's proud of the way I earned it. She wouldn't." I leave no room for argument because while the rest of the world may know Scarlet Kingston as an ice queen, she's an amazing mom, and she'd never do this to me.

"Care to make a wager?" he asks in typical Maddox fashion.

Like I said before . . . he's a cocky fucker.

"Sure. You ready to lose?" I cross my legs and sit my barely touched drink on the bar. "What are the stakes?"

This isn't our first bet. We've been betting each other for as long as I can remember.

"If I win, I get the penthouse."

"No," I laugh. "No chance. That's our penthouse."

"*Your* penthouse, Brynn. Lindy and Everly are both married. Gracie's going back to London once she's done rehabbing her foot, and Kenzie's residency has her in DC for the next few years. You don't need all that space to yourself. And anyway . . . if you're so sure I'm wrong, what's it gonna hurt?" He's also done this before. Played some form of chicken with me. He knows I hate backing down. I hate being challenged almost as much as losing.

"Fine. If you win, we swap condos. But if *I win*, I want the 'Stang."

He recoils like he just took a punch to the gut from my brother, who fights in a cage for a living. Madman's 1966 cherry-red Mustang convertible is in mint condition with a white soft-top and shiny white rims. The engine purrs prettier than anything I've ever heard, and I have a thing for cars. It's a classic, and I've loved it since the very first time he drove to my house to pick me up in it.

"Done." He offers me his hand, and a chill runs down my spine.

I should probably be scared of how easily he just agreed. Maddox loves that car more than anything. He must be sure he can win this one. But there's no way I'm losing. My mom knows how much I love my job. She knows how hard I worked for it. And after these past few months, she knows exactly what it means to me. She wouldn't just force me to switch teams in a way she'd never force another physical therapist to do. She just wouldn't.

"I'm going to look so good driving your baby, Madman." I take another small sip of my drink and smile before Callen waves Maddox down to his end of the bar.

The fucker turns to me and smirks. "Enjoy your delusions, Brynnie."

He slides out of his spot, and I turn back to the bar and wave down Lou. "Could I get a Coke?"

"Rum and Coke?" Lou checks, and I shake my head.

"Just Coke, please."

"She won't say no to a few cherries in it though."

I whip my head around to see who the hell just slipped into Maddox's space and nearly swallow my tongue.

"Deacon?" I gasp, shocked to see the boy Lindy and I used to drool over as teenagers. I haven't seen him since the last time my family visited Block Island and stayed at the inn his family owns on the coast. Only the man sitting next to me is twice the size and at least ten years older than the boy I last saw.

Lou places my soda in front of me, and Deacon reaches across the bar and swipes two cherries to drop in my glass. "How are you doing, red?"

Deacon

*L*ittle Brynlee St. James isn't so little anymore, but she blushes the same way she used to when we were kids.

With her entire face.

And fuck me.

She's got a beautiful face.

Tiny freckles dot the bridge of her nose, tinged pink from too much sun. Strawberry-blonde hair hangs down over bare shoulders, dancing against porcelain skin. And those green eyes . . . Emerald green. Greener than the greenest grass I've ever seen. Eyes that used to watch me every single summer are staring at me now, making my dick harder than it's been in a damn decade. Brynlee fucking St. James.

Guess I knew I'd be running into her sooner or later.

But I didn't expect it to be tonight.

"Cat got your tongue?" I tease when she sits silently, stunned. "You never used to stop talking. You and your cousin, and that little sister. *Lilly?*" I ask.

"Livvy," she smiles. "Lindy is technically my aunt, not my cousin, and Livvy is my sister. But she started college and wants to be called Olivia now." She tilts her head and just looks at me for a moment, her eyes scanning my face, then down my chest before coming back up. I don't miss the way her flush deepens and her lips part. "What are you doing here, Deacon?"

"I promised my daughter I'd spend the day on the beach with her. Her mom and stepdad have a place down here for the week. My friend, Ripley, rents a house down here in the offseason. He was supposed to meet me here tonight. I was looking for him when I found you."

Now I'm thinking I might just blow off Rip.

Hell . . . he'll understand.

She nods her head slowly while she plays with one of the cherries I dropped in her soda. "Right. I heard you had a little girl."

"Yeah. Kennedy. She's a spitfire. Her mom always brings her down here for her birthday." My kid's got us all wrapped around her little finger. All of us.

She pops the cherry in her mouth, then pulls the stem out —tied in a knot—a few seconds later, then drops it on the damp napkin sitting under her drink. Everything about the move is sexy, but Brynlee looks like she's completely oblivious to her sex appeal as she smiles almost shyly up at me. "We're actually down for my best friends' birthdays too. Guess they're in good company."

"Guess they are," I agree and look at the stem, laughing. "You remember the summer you were determined to learn how to do that?"

She giggles. "What were we? Thirteen?"

"*You* might have been. Pretty sure I was sixteen or seventeen." I think back to that summer. The last one before I left for college. It was the last summer I saw her for a few years. And the next time I came home, Brynn didn't look like a little girl anymore. But she was still jailbait. Something her dad made sure I knew—more than once. Cade may have thought he was being nonchalant about it, but when a former MMA champion makes sure you know exactly how old, or more precisely how young, his daughter is, you don't forget it.

"Yeah . . . I guess you were." She stirs her soda and looks up at me through long lashes. "So I heard you left Boston University. Do you have a new coaching job lined up?"

"Guess you haven't heard the news yet. I think it's being announced at some point next week."

Her nose crinkles in a way that shouldn't be sexy but is. "What's being announced?"

She pops another cherry into her mouth and closes those pouty pink lips around it.

"Your family just hired me as the Revolution's new head coach."

BRYNLEE

I suck in a quick, shocked breath and accidentally inhale a cherry. The little fucker slips right down my throat and lodges there until I'm a coughing, choking mess. Deacon pounds my back like a baseball player excited for a teammate's homerun until I manage to force up the cherry and spit it into a napkin, *like the lady my mother raised me to be.*

Scarlet Kingston-St. James would die if she saw what I just did.

"I'm sorry." I wipe the tears from my eyes, pretty sure they're there from the coughing and not the mortification. At least that's what I'm going to tell myself. "Could you repeat that?"

A slow, sexy smile stretches along Deacon's full lips.

Why are guys always blessed with good lips and long lashes?

This man has had both since he was fifteen.

It wasn't fair then, and it's certainly not fair now.

"The back pounding?" That smile turns cocky and does things to me it absolutely should not. "I mean . . . if that's what you're into, I'm not gonna judge."

Damn him, because suddenly that's what I'd like to be into.

Any kind of pounding that involves this man sounds good to me.

I snicker to myself. *Pounding.* I have the sense of humor of a teenage boy.

Instead of admitting that, I cross my legs, going more for sexy and less for choking, and try to get control of my racing thoughts, like that's possible. It may have worked, too, if Deacon's eyes didn't catch on my thighs while my shorts ride up on my legs. But there's no missing the way those eyes darken as he takes in the view.

Some women may be body conscious, but I'm not one of them. I've trained at my father's gym for what feels like every day of my life, and it's given me a level of confidence that nothing else ever has. It doesn't hurt that it's also given me black belts in judo and Brazilian jiu jitsu. And I'm trained in Maui Thai. But I keep that to myself and gently tap him with the toe of my crossed foot. "My eyes are up here, Kane."

"We going with last names, St. James?" He leans back against the bar, confident and relaxed and so damn sexy, as if I didn't just hack up a cherry like a hair ball after he told me he was taking over my team two minutes ago.

My. Team.

The one I love.

The one I fought to be a respected part of.

The one I had to prove I deserved to work for.

He can't be coaching my team.

I'd have heard about that. *Wouldn't I?*

I think back to my conversation with Maddox.

Could this have anything to do with him thinking I'm being switched to the Philadelphia Kings? Maybe he misunderstood what he heard and really it was something about this.

I drag myself back to the conversation at hand and try to keep us at this teasing level before I lose my shit completely. "I don't know. Should I be calling you Coach Kane?"

I remember watching him play when we were young.

The way he moved. Like he was one with the ice . . . He was beautiful.

He only got one year playing in the pros before he blew out his knee and never got back to the game. I remember reading that he took the job as an assistant coach at Boston University the following year. Thanks to poor choices by the existing head coach involving a coed, Deacon was promoted to head coach two years later. My best friends' younger brother Nixon played for him. I guess he's about to again.

I can't believe my family just hired him.

Deacon has the decency to look uncomfortable for a flash of a moment before his smile slips back into place. "Not yet. It's not official for a few more days." He looks around us at the crowd of people. No one seems to be paying us any attention, but they're there, and they're definitely close enough to be hearing our conversation. "I probably shouldn't have even mentioned it. Not here, at least."

"Not exactly a great place to talk without getting caught," I agree, just as a body knocks me forward. I reach out and steady myself with a hand against Deacon's chest as a rowdy guy who smells like he's had one too many beers spilled on him knocks into me again.

Deacon immediately shifts, pulling me against him. "Watch it, man. Keep your fucking hands to yourself," he growls with a low, sexy voice that makes my knees weak and my panties damp.

But Deacon was always good at that.

When I was younger, I had such a crush on him.

He was big, broad, and filled out his board shorts so damn nicely. But holy hell . . . teenage Deacon doesn't hold a candle to the man standing in front of me. And that voice . . . that growl . . . they just put my memories to shame because that was way hotter than it should have been.

But when the drunk guy steps up to Deacon and has to lift his head up, and up, and up a little further, just to look him in the eyes, well . . . yeah. I can't control my laugh. Because Coach Kane is six six and this guy might be five eight. And where Deacon is broad with what I'd bet is very little fat on his body, this guy looks like he's never met a beer he hasn't slammed.

There's no comparison.

"Whatever, asshole," sloppy drunk mumbles loud enough for us to hear, and Deacon's eyes go absolutely feral.

I grab the front of his shirt and stop him from taking a step toward the guy. "He's not worth it, and you're about to be way too high profile to be bothered by that man, Kane."

He takes a step closer to me, essentially blocking me off from everyone else with his big body, and a chill skirts down my spine from our closeness. "He didn't even apologize." Deacon bends his knees to close the distance between us, bringing our faces inches apart. "He's not a man. He's a coward, Brynlee."

I drop my hand and look away because suddenly this feels a little too intimate, with a man I barely know as I sit on a barstool in O'Malley's.

I'm not sure what to do with that because I don't think I want it to stop.

"Hey." He lifts my chin, and the connection zings and zaps between us like an electric current. "Where'd you go there?"

I shake my head, trying to clear my thoughts and say the first thing that comes to mind. "Do you know how big of a crush I had on you as a kid?"

When Deacon smiles this time, *it's different.*

This time, it reaches the depths of his nearly navy-blue eyes.

"It was pretty hard to miss it, if you want the truth." He tucks a lock of hair behind my ear, then twirls it around his thick finger, and I melt . . . literally melt into a pile of goo.

"Oh yeah?" I ask quietly and catch my bottom lip between my teeth as he moves his face closer to mine. "You never said anything."

"Come on, Brynlee. You were too young." His eyes dart between mine, and he tugs that lock of hair, sending a quick hit of longing straight through me. "And when you finally weren't too young, your dad made sure I knew in his eyes, you still were."

Yeah . . . I kinda had a feeling Dad did that, based on a conversation I overheard once between him, Uncle Sam, and Uncle Becks.

I could blame what I do next on the shot of whiskey from earlier, or my extra strong margarita, but either would be a lie.

In fact, what I'm about to do is something I wanted to do every single summer we vacationed on Block Island. Something Lindy heard me babble on and on about each year.

I reach up and drag my thumb over Deacon's bottom lip.

The one I dreamed about kissing back when I didn't have any idea how good kissing a boy could be, let alone a man. "I'm not too young now."

Deacon

This woman is dangerous.

Her thumb drags along my lower lip as her teeth assault her own pouty, glossed smile.

I'm not a man who wants much. But *fuck* . . . I want her.

"Brynlee . . . I'm signing a contract this week to work for your family for the next five years." I thumb her soft, silky tresses between my fingers, and swear to God, all my blood rushes to my cock.

She nods slowly with a sinful smile on her pretty face. "You are." Her words are slow and nearly whispered in the loud bar, but there's no missing them. "Not that they've told me, but I'm taking your word for it."

Her knees brush my thigh as she leans in impossibly close.

Close enough I can smell a hint of tequila and lime on her warm breath as it pulls me in. "But did you know . . ." She sucks in a quick, short breath as her leg brushes gently against my erection. Wide green eyes fly to mine before they focus, and she tries to school her delicate features. Pouty pink glossed lips form the prettiest little O for a split-second before she smooths her expression. "The organization doesn't have a no fraternization policy. They really couldn't. My family members are masters at nepotism and fraternization." I'm not even sure she realizes she's laughing. "In fact, my Uncle Max married Aunt Daphne right after he promoted her from his assistant to running the Revolution's charity foundation."

"Is that so?" I lean my hands on either side of the bar behind her, effectively caging her in, and damn . . . there go those wide eyes again.

Suddenly, the fearless girl who used to follow me around is looking back at me, and the rest of the room disappears around us.

"It is," she whispers against my lips.

Tempting me to taste her.

Teasing the strength of my restraint.

I wasn't expecting Brynlee St. James tonight.

"You here with anyone, Brynlee?" My fingers flex tensely against the bar, the wood beneath my grasp threatening to splinter with the strength it's taking me to resist touching her.

"No . . ." Her eyes dart to the side, looking around quickly. "Just a few cousins. But we'll all find our way home. Why? Do you want to get out of here?" Something like excitement dances in her glittering emerald eyes.

"Not really my scene," I groan back as her knee grazes my dick again.

She's got to know what she's doing, but if she does, she sure as hell isn't letting on. Instead, she pulls a pink polka-dotted phone from the pocket of tiny white shorts that show off beautifully sculpted thighs. Her thumbs fly across the screen before she hops off the stool and steps into my chest.

Damn, this woman is tiny, barely coming up mid-chest.

But what she lacks in height, she's definitely making up for in sass.

She always did.

"You ready to go, Kane?"

I flex my fingers against the bar once more in the time it takes me to make a split-second decision. *Fuck.* This is probably a bad idea, but for the life of me, I don't seem to care right now.

Shy never was my thing anyway.

The little spitfire ducks down under my arm, then flips her hair and looks over her shoulder before she bats long black lashes at me. "You coming, Kane?"

Like there was ever a chance I'd say no. "Lead the way, St. James."

BRYNLEE

**Classy women don't have one-night stands.
That was an audition.
Either you made the cut or you didn't.**

—Brynlee's Secret Thoughts

The faintest hint of sun barely begins to peek out beyond the horizon as Deacon and I lie on the cool sand, resting on bent elbows against the dunes. Hours have passed while we caught each other up on the past decade, although *caught up* feels wrong. Teenage me never really knew Deacon Kane. She may have fantasized about him from afar, a time or ten, but she never really got the chance to know the boy who became this man.

In fact, I'm fairly certain teenage me would lose her actual shit if she could see me now.

Back then, I fantasized about what it would be like to spend a night with Deacon.

I looked forward to the few weeks a year we'd spend on Block Island because I knew I could indulge in a few weeks away from Kroydon Hills and all the prying eyes that were interested in our lives just because of who our parents are. But I also got to spend a few weeks imagining myself flirting with the boy Deacon used to be. *Imagining* being the key word. I didn't even know how to flirt back then. It's hard to learn how to act with teenage boys when they only ever cared about the fact that my dad was Cade St. James, former MMA champion. Wait ... that's not completely true. Some of them thought the fact that my mom owns the Philadelphia Kings was cool too. Those guys usually wanted to meet my friends though, because their dad was the Kings quarterback.

And now I sound like a poor little rich girl. Even to myself.

Deacon was different. He never had stars in his eyes over my parents.

Unfortunately, he never had stars in his eyes for me either.

He was too old and too cool for me back then, so none of it made much of a difference.

Now, here we are, talking about all the ways our twenties have kicked our collective asses. Not that I've shared *all* the ways, but I've shared a whole lot more than I thought I would. And that single thought is like a strike to the chest, stealing the breath from my lungs.

I try to focus on the here and now.

On the cool sand and the hot man.

On the serenity around me.

Not on the uncertain future and what it holds for me.

I lift my eyes to the heavens and take it all in. "I don't remember the last time I watched the sun rise."

"Me either. Now all-nighters only happen if Kennedy is sick. This kind of peace is few and far between," he muses.

Peace . . . I desperately long to remember what that's like.

The soft, warm, water-colored rays reflect off the dark water beneath them, gently illuminating the ocean, and slowly stretch over the beach. I lower my elbows and lie back on the sand as I soak in the beauty. "It's gorgeous."

"It is," he answers. But when I glance his way, he's looking at me, not the ocean. And what could be a cheesy line coming from someone else spreads goosebumps over my skin coming from Deacon.

I roll to my side and face this man I haven't seen in nearly a decade, and yet feel inexplicably comfortable with, and try to smother another yawn as it creeps up on me, *again*.

I know our night is coming to an end.

Figuratively and literally.

"I should probably get back to the house soon." I force the words out, wishing I could stop time.

"Are you down here all week?" Deacon asks as he mirrors my body.

Close enough to feel his warmth but not close enough to feel *him*.

It seems to have been a theme tonight.

Flirting but not acting.

Close but not quite close enough.

With a sudden strong wave of disappointment draining me, I slowly shake my head. "No. I'm heading back to Kroydon Hills later this morning. I've got a few appointments on the schedule tomorrow with some of the guys. Should I send you a report, Coach?" The teasing rolls off my tongue, and Deacon's lips curl into a crooked, sexy grin.

"Not sure if my email is set up yet, St. James." He rises slowly and brushes the sand from well-worn jeans, then bends his knees and offers me his hands.

"Guess it's time to go, huh?" I rest my hands in his big palms and let him pull me to my feet before I look up into his eyes. "Are you going to be down here for long . . . ? Do you have to do the whole find a place to live thing? I mean, now that you're relocating from Boston to Philly. Where are you staying? When are you moving?"

Deacon ignores my rapid-fire questions and runs both big hands over my head before he wraps one around the back of my neck and drags a rough thumb along my jaw. My body immediately slows and takes notice. "Anyone ever told you, you talk too much?"

I scrunch my face and purse my lips, like I have to think about my answer.

I don't.

I've been told I talk too much for years.

When I shrug in response, he drops his hand and takes a step back.

Damn it. I'm not sure I've ever been so disappointed at the loss of someone's hands on my body, and it wasn't even like that.

"I've got a meeting with the Kings again tomorrow, so I'm heading back today too."

And the other shoe dropped.

"The Kings . . ." I cock my head and watch him for any reaction. "You mean my mother?" I half tease, half taunt because I'm not sure how to feel about him meeting with my mother and uncle. It's amazing how easy it was to forget who we were talking about.

He bends his knees until he's at my eye level. "Hey . . . where'd you go there?"

"Just remembering you're basically my boss," I confess sheepishly and take a small step back.

"I'm not your boss yet." Deacon closes the space between us, and for one single second, I think he might kiss me. He lifts his hand to my face but drops it before he touches me.

"I'm in Room 210 at the Kroydon Hill Plaza. Have dinner with me tonight."

His words wage war in my mind, but when I open my mouth to answer him, my own words get stuck in my throat.

"Don't answer now." He reaches his hand into my pocket and pulls out my phone, then unlocks it with my face before his fingers fly across the screen, and before I can over-analyze what just happened, he hands it back to me. "I should be home by seven tonight. You've got my number. You've got the hotel information. Use it, Brynn."

I nod slowly and pocket my phone, then motion toward the house behind us. "That's me."

Deacon clenches his jaw and shoves his hand in his pocket. "Room 210, Brynn. You've got to eat."

The gleam in his eye is intense as the sun casts a golden glow behind him.

"Room 210," I whisper back before I force myself to turn around and head for my parents' house.

I quietly let myself in and tip toe down the hall to the kitchen, expecting it to be empty. Looks like nothing is going to go my way today though. Because instead of finding an empty kitchen, Maddox is standing shirtless behind the island, twisting the cap off a bottle of water.

Fuck me.

He grins and takes a pull of water. "Looks like little red didn't sleep in her bed."

"Pretty sure you're mixing up fairytales, Madman." I maneuver around him and grab my own water from the fridge. "What are you doing up?"

"Going for a run," he tells me, and his grin turns into a full-on ferocious smile. "And I may have needed to escort a guest out this morning. I swear to fuck, I don't understand why women want to spend the night. Do you all really think we want to wake up next to you and watch you do the walk of shame? You won't catch a man doing that. We get the fuck out before the sun comes up for a reason."

"What is wrong with you?" I pull myself up to sit on the counter next to him. "Did Uncle Sam drop you as a baby?"

"Listen, she had fake lashes stuck to her cheeks like a goddamn caterpillar this morning. I almost tried to kill one before I realized what it was." Maddox crosses his arms over his chest and stares at me, daring me to question him. Not like there's any way in hell I'm going to. I learned a long time ago I don't want to know what Maddox and Callen do behind closed doors.

Hell, I'm not so sure they haven't shared women before.

And with that thought, my stomach sours.

Eww.

"Whatever, Madman. I'm going to bed." I hop down to leave but stop cold when my phone vibrates.

Did Deacon take my number when he gave me his?

I pull it from my pocket and see two text notifications.

One is from Deacon. It looks like he did text himself from my phone.

Sneaky fucker.

The other is from my mom.

> MOM
>
> Good morning, Brynn. I need you to come by the house today.

"Awful early for a text, B."

I glare at Maddox.

He's not wrong.

After a minute wasted staring at my phone, I decide to call my mother. Scarlet Kingston-St. James doesn't know how to sleep late. She never has, as she just demonstrated by texting at the crack of dawn... literally.

It barely rings before she answers, and out of the corner of my eye, I catch Maddox grabbing an apple from the fruit bowl and pull up a stool. Like I said, such a fucker.

"Hey, sweetheart. I didn't expect you to be awake so early on a Sunday." I hear coffee beans grinding in the background before she must move out of the kitchen. "How are you feeling?"

"I was fine until I got your message, Mom. What's going on, and why do I feel like I'm being summoned?"

Maddox pulls his pocketknife from his shorts and cuts a slice of his apple while I roll my eyes at my audience. One of these days, he's going to slice his mouth open with the way he bites the damn thing right off the blade. And when that day comes, I'm going to laugh before I faint from the excessive amount of blood.

"Don't be dramatic, Brynn. You're not being summoned. I just want to discuss something with you." Well she certainly brought my attention right back to her.

"Discuss what?" I question as my stomach sinks and I glare at my cousin.

No way was he right.

She wouldn't do that to me.

"If I wanted to discuss it over the phone, I would have called you, Brynlee," my mother chastises, like I'm a child.

"I have things to do today, Mom. I'm not even in Kroydon Hills. What's going on?" I ask a little firmer this time.

Maddox coughs, and I glance his way quickly.

And suddenly it feels like the my world is shifting.

Holy. Hell.

He was right.

"It's a business thing, honey. Just come over for lunch or

dinner, and we'll discuss it then." My mother isn't used to being told no.

In her defense, she's almost always right, so it doesn't have to happen often.

In my defense, it's about to happen now.

"You're not really going to try to make me switch from the Revolution to the Kings, are you, Mom?" My shaking voice betrays any confidence I was attempting to project. "You wouldn't do that to me, would you? You know I love my job. You know how hard I work. You wouldn't go behind my back and pull rank . . . right?"

"Brynlee, I don't have to pull rank. I'm the vice president of King Corp. I'm the GM of the Philadelphia Kings and part owner of the Philadelphia Revolution. I *am* the rank someone wants to pull. I want to discuss this with you in person. Come to the house."

"Mom—"

"The Kings will be better for your health, Brynn. The season's shorter, and there's less travel. You know I'm right."

I grip my phone as the anger coursing through my veins threatens to engulf me. "Are you kidding me?"

"Brynlee—"

"I'll save you the hassle, Mom. Consider this my notice. My contract says I have to give you a month. Today is day one."

I end the call and turn back to Maddox, who's grinning like the wolf from *Little Red Riding Hood*. "Looks like it's a good day for a move."

I rip the apple out of his hand and throw it at his head. "Fuck you, Maddox."

The son of a bitch ducks. "Better go shower, Brynn. Looks like you've got some news to break to Gracie."

"You know you're a dick, right?"

He shrugs. "A dick with a penthouse condo."

Did I really just lose my job and my home in one day?

BRYNLEE

**Congratulations! You've successfully made it to the end of June.
Welcome to the next level of *Jumanji*.**

—Brynlee's Secret Thoughts

I begrudgingly let Maddox and Callen convince me to pick up cinnamon rolls from our favorite beach town bakery later that morning. Sugar and coffee is the easiest way to the twins' hearts, and I'm about to tell Everly and Gracie that Gracie and I are swapping condos with Tweedle Dee and Tweedle Whore, so I need all the help I can get.

I walk ahead of Callen and Maddox, pissed at them.
Pissed at myself.
Pissed at my mom.
Basically, pissed at the world.
It's too early to be this angry.

At least until Everly's husband, Cross, opens the door, and their one-year-old son, Jax, runs between his legs, playing peek-a-boo. An utterly exhausted-looking Cross scoops him up and pushes the door wide open as he groans, "Hey, Brynn. They're on the back deck."

I lean over and kiss Jax on the cheek, then walk through the house, dodging big, fat, neon Legos meant to do severe damage to bare feet and slightly slutty-looking dolls that remind me of a few too many nights in college spent doing things I may be less than proud of but luckily don't completely remember.

It's official. I'd say I should go back to bed, but that would imply I'd been there already today, and that hasn't happened yet. *Fuck*. It's going to be a long, damn day.

Gracie and Everly both look up in sync with their nearly identical faces as I drop the sweets on the table.

Everly cocks a brow in question as Gracie very carefully lifts the blue bakery box lid, then looks at me. "What did you do that you're bribing me with sweets, Brynnie?"

What did I do? I should tell her I made a deal with the devil, but I may be questioning whether said devil is my mother or my cousin.

Fucking Maddox.

"So . . ." I pull out a chair and sit down, pulling a knee up to my chest and wrapping an arm around my bare leg after I adjust my shorts.

Apparently, I take too long to answer, though, because Maddox and Callen have joined me outside, and Satan opens his big, fat mouth first. "Listen." He grabs a cinnamon roll and takes a bite. *I love my cousin. Really, I do. But in this moment, I may be wishing for him to choke . . . just a tiny bit.* "Callen and I are going to swap condos with Brynn. She doesn't need all that space anymore, but we could use it. So you'll be moving into our condo." He takes another bite and then turns his traitorous grin on me. "See? Wasn't that hard."

"I'm getting coffee," Callen grumbles, getting the hell out of the line of fire, and Everly laughs while I contemplate both their deaths.

Okay, maybe not deaths, but I could go for a good maiming.

I think that's called for.

"It's decaf..." Everly calls after him in a melodic voice that's way too chipper for this early.

"Fuck," he mutters as he disappears into the kitchen, and Maddox takes the small distraction as an opening and sits down in the seat next to me.

My eye twitches while I try to fight the urge to stab him with the plastic fork he's using to eat the cinnamon roll I paid for.

Meanwhile, Gracie is staring at me like I've lost my mind. Which might not be too far off at this point. "Did you just *Friends* us?" she finally asks, much calmer than I deserve for her to be, but that's Gracie. Always the calm one. Always the peacemaker and people pleaser. I'm not even sure if she's asking me or Maddox, but neither of us deserves her calm right now. "Because there's no way you'd give up that condo for theirs. Is there?"

"Don't ask," I murmur as I stuff an entire pastry in my mouth, then shove one her way. "Try them," I tell her around a mouth full of food. "They're good."

Everly laughs so hard, I think Gracie might actually kick her leg under the table to shut her up, but Everly doesn't care. "Dude. You're going to be sleeping where so many women have slept before. I hope you clean that place with bleach before you touch any surfaces. Seriously, girls. Beware of STDs. I bet some of them are even airborne."

I turn my head slowly to my cousin with an uncontrollable twitch in my eye and hiss, "I fucking hate you."

Maddox just grins, baring his teeth like the psycho he likes to pretend he is, and after this, I'm inclined to believe him.

"Honest to God, one of you had better tell me what I missed," Gracie tries to demand, but it falls on deaf ears when we both ignore her.

Everly picks up Gracie's phone with a little too much glee, and Grace finally glares. "What the hell are you doing?"

"Door Dashing bleach to your new condo. You're gonna need a lot of it."

"Time to wake up, Brynn."

My eyes fly open, startled by Callen's voice, and I look around to get my bearings. "Sorry," I mumble when I realize I'm in his Escalade in the parking garage under our condos back in Kroydon Hills. I'd caught a ride down to the beach with Maddox, but there was no way in hell I was riding back home with him. Leaving Callen as the lesser of two evils. At least for today.

He and I have always been close. Hell, at one point I thought maybe it could have been more. But Callen spent most of college with his high school sweetheart, and once they broke up during his senior year, he's spent time with every other woman who's smiled at him since. I guess it's safe to say I got over any thought of an us because we're way better as friends than we would have been as anything else.

"I hadn't realized I fell asleep," I manage to say around a yawn.

"You passed out as soon as we got on the AC Expressway. Late night last night?"

I close my eyes and picture the sunrise, trying to get back some of that peace from this morning. Only instead of picturing the sun, an image of a handsome man with piercing blue eyes fills my memory and warms my cheeks. "Something like that."

We get out of the SUV, and he grabs my bag and his. Callen might be one of the biggest manwhores I know, but he's always been a gentleman . . . At least where I'm concerned. Not sure many women would say the same.

"You're really not gonna tell me why we're swapping condos?" he pushes, having asked the same question a handful of times already.

I glance over at Maddox's still-empty parking spot and get ragey again. "Ask your roommate."

I'm not ready to talk about this.

Not with him.

Not with anyone.

I'm not even sure I'm ready to talk to my mom, and I know that needs to happen sooner rather than later. She isn't one to ever accept being ignored. Not from her children. Not from anyone. My family might be full of kings, but she's the queen we all bow down to.

"Whatever." Callen chuckles half-heartedly as he nudges me to walk ahead of him. "Your loss is my gain."

Yeah, I guess it is.

Maddox wasn't wrong this morning. The penthouse is too big for just me. There used to be five of us rooming together. And as of a few weeks ago, it's just me now. Gracie's here for the summer, but she's going back to London after we get her rehabbed. Maybe I just need to put a positive spin on this. Maybe . . . it was meant to be.

Whatever.

There aren't enough cinnamon rolls in the world to help convince myself of that bullshit today. Maybe I'll try again tomorrow.

We stop at the coffee shop on the first floor of our building, and I try to prepare myself for the rest of this shit show of a day. Two large coffees, one bacon, egg, and cheese bagel for Callen, and a banana for me later, and the two of us head upstairs.

Might as well get this over with.

"You really not going to talk to me?" Maddox grabs my elbow as I walk past him with my last armful of clothes dangling from velvet hangers. A girl's got to have some vices, and one of the very few I have is designer clothes. It just happens to be a very expensive vice.

We've been at this swap for hours, and as I've packed things up, it's become even more obvious that I really didn't need this much space. Not anymore.

But still . . .

Knowing the place was too big and knowing I lost it in a bet are two totally different beasts. Kinda like my cousin. And I'm not happy with either thought at this particular moment.

I lock my eyes on Maddox, glaring daggers, then slowly drag them between the two of us, down to where his hand holds my elbow, silently demanding him to let go and feeling immensely proud of myself for not stomping on his foot like I desperately want to do. Mentally, I may revert back to a five-year-old, but physically, I stand my ground, refusing to give him any ammunition.

"You're going to have to talk to me at some point, Brynnie."

"Do. Not. *Brynnie* me." Fury runs rampant through my veins.

I don't know who I'm more angry with. Him, my mom, or myself.

He presses his palm flat against the wall, blocking my path. "I won the bet, fair and square. What do you want from me?"

I lose the internal battle and throw an elbow into his side, then walk by. "I wanted you to tell me what you knew when you found out and not have used it against me in a bet. That was a shitty thing to do, Madman."

"Brynn..."

I walk away, leaving him behind.

I'll get over this. He and I have made a million bets in our lifetime.

But I sure as hell won't be getting over it today.

My family owns this building, and half my cousins and I moved in once we moved out of our parents' houses. So between my family and the twins' family all helping, we get everything moved pretty quickly.

As quickly as you can pack up an entire penthouse.

But they're all giving me a pretty wide birth.

No one ever said the Kingstons were stupid.

And anyone who's ever met my mother's generation should watch out. Because my cousins and I, the second generation of Kingstons, are even closer than the first. We put our parents to shame. That's probably the only reason I haven't already castrated Maddox.

Stupid family loyalty.

Grace has been quiet throughout the day. She knows I'm

hiding something, but she won't push it. I'm pretty sure she's hiding something too, so I'm just going to go with it.

Hours later, once it's just Gracie and me in the guys' old condo, which I still refuse to call *our* new condo, I decide rage-cleaning may be the best way to channel my anger. It's either that or going to Crucible, Dad's gym, to sweat it out, and cleaning feels more productive.

"You're really not going to spill the beans?" Grace asks from the other side of the modern kitchen that looks like it's barely been used for anything other than takeout in the years since the guys moved in.

"Listen," I stop her as I yank my green and pink rubber gloves up to my elbows and dump out the cleaning supplies on the shiny black granite counter. It's masculine and cold and not at all like the pretty white and gray marble we'd picked out for the penthouse years ago. *Stupid counter.* "It doesn't matter. What matters now is that *this* is the new condo, and I'm so excited you're here with me for the summer, Grace. Now grab a pair of gloves and get cleaning. This place smells like Callen's dirty gym socks."

I was always the neat freak out of the five of us. I like to keep my life organized, and if my house is unorganized, my life feels chaotic. And I hate chaos.

Once she realizes I'm not kidding, Gracie pulls on a pair of purple gloves with a satisfying snap. "Whatever you say, crazy lady."

I'm not being fair to her, and I know it.

Damn it.

Being mean to Grace is like kicking the cutest puppy dog ever.

And I can't do it.

"Listen, it just made sense. That's all. You're only staying a few weeks, and I don't need a five-bedroom condo all to myself. You've all moved out and moved on, and I'm the only one left here. So please help me make this place livable."

I pass her a bucket filled with bathroom cleaning supplies and smile when she groans.

"Seriously?" she basically whines. "Can't we hire someone to do this?"

I spray the granite countertop, then look up at her and snap a little. "Sure, we can hire someone. And while we're waiting for them to get here, you can tell me what the hell is going on with you and the god of war because we haven't had five minutes alone to talk since you got back. And you better believe I didn't miss the fact that you two showed up together."

Gracie showed up at Everly's beach house, having flown home from London with Everly's brother-in-law, Ares. And the tension coming off them in waves was enough to light up the entire city.

Grace blushes, totally busted but unwilling to have this conversation, which is perfectly fine with me. "Fine. I'll scrub the damn bathroom."

"Bathrooms, Grace." I wait with both brows raised, then smile. "There's two of them."

"I hate you," she grumbles as she walks away.

"We're still going to talk about it, good twin," I call after her, because while I might be in no shape to have this conversation right now, we're going to have this conversation at some point. I might have had a shit day, but Gracie and Everly have been two of my best friends since I was three years old. And there's definitely something going on with good twin that she's hiding.

By the time I've got the kitchen clean enough that I'm not afraid to put my dishes into the cabinets, my arms hurt from exertion, but it's a good kind of pain. At least that's what I'm telling myself as I stand back and appreciate the shine of the streak-free stainless-steel appliances.

GRACE

You are disgusting.

EVERLY

You're going to need to be more specific, Gracie.

KENZIE

Ohh . . . Who's disgusting?

GRACE

Oops. I sent this to the wrong chat. Hold please.

Okay, Callen and Maddox have now been added to the chat.

LINDY

Dude. Make sure you remove their asses after this. I don't want to talk about sucking my husband's dick with the guys on the text.

MADDOX

WTF? I don't want to know that shit.

CALLEN

Sweet. Let's hear it.

EVERLY

What is wrong with you?

CALLEN

I'm not related to her and she's HOT AF. Come on, Lindy. Let's hear it.

LINDY

Is this why they're disgusting?

MADDOX

Whose disgusting?

GRACE

You! When was the last time you assholes cleaned?

BRYNLEE

Better question - Why don't you have a cleaning lady?

KENZIE

Wait . . . I know the answer. Callen fucked her, then called her the wrong name.

EVERLY

OMG. Seriously? Your balls are going to shrivel up from some dirty disease, Callen.

CALLEN

I wrap it up every single time. Thank you very much.

GRACE

And that's why you're gross. I found your condoms.

CALLEN

Safe sex, good twin. You should try it.

GRACE

THEY WERE USED!

EVERLY

OMG.

LINDY

Shame on your house!

KENZIE

. . . I just threw up in my mouth.

CALLEN

But did you swallow?

KENZIE

I fucking hate you.

MADDOX

You're a doctor. You've seen worse.

BRYNLEE

I hate you too.

Callen Did you happen to find any unused condoms, Grace? I was looking for my box while we were unpacking.

Callen has been removed from the conversation.

LINDY

Get rid of Maddox too.

Maddox has been removed from the conversation.

EVERLY

Good. Never let them in our sacred space again.

BRYNLEE

Okay, Mother Earth.

The Philly Press

KROYDON KRONICLES

DIRTY DEETS & HOCKEY HOTTIES

Could summer in the city be heating up? Word is spreading that Philly's favorite hockey team has added a new hockey hottie to their roster. But wait . . . is the Revolution's newest addition a player or a coach? Rumors are circulating they've been in talks to replace their newly retired, multi-Cup-winning coach with a hot, young newcomer to the pros. So young, he may just be the youngest coach ever to coach pro hockey. And this reporter is ready to dig up the truth of it all. Stay tuned for all the dirty deets, peeps.

#KroydonKronicles

DEACON

"I thought your new position was being kept quiet until you officially signed your new contract this week."

I'm suddenly glad to be having this conversation via Bluetooth instead of in person, because at least this way I can't get shit for the look on my face as I navigate the sweltering streets of Kroydon Hills, listening to my ex-wife—who happens to be one of my best friends—manage to nag me as if she were my current wife. But instead of showing her any of that, I just nod in agreement.

"Yeah, so did I. I'm sure the Kingston's PR team already has someone on it. Just ignore that trash, Isla. It's not news. It's gossip." Some shithead kid slams on the horn of his Tesla that Mommy and Daddy probably bought him as I stop at the yellow light instead of running it, and I flip him the fuck off, already done with today. "I don't know why you read those things in the first place. They're called gossip rags for a reason." After a moment, the light turns green, and I turn into the parking lot of the Kroydon Hills Plaza, wishing I hadn't had to leave Isla, her husband, Shaun, and our daughter, Kennedy, at the beach for a few more days. "Seriously, why are you even following the *Kroydon Kronicles* anyway?"

"I don't follow them," she clucks, her words dripping with annoyance. "I have notifications set up for your name, and I added the Revolution after your meeting last week. Someone has to look out for you, Deacon. You're not very good at doing it yourself." Her voice holds a condescending tone, like I just asked the most ridiculous question Isla's ever heard. Her tolerance for having to explain herself has never been one of her better qualities. At least, not with anyone who isn't our daughter. Her husband and I have had a few beers and laughed over her lack of patience more than once at her expense.

The four of us don't have what most would consider a stereotypical blended-family relationship.

When she and I got divorced, our relationship actually got better, not worse. Which was a good thing. If we'd continued down the path we'd been on for much longer, things would have gotten ugly. We somehow managed to end our marriage as friends who are able to put Kennedy first.

The late afternoon sun bakes against the truck's windshield as I choose my next words carefully. "Listen . . . News is going to spread. There's nothing we can do about that. If anyone reaches out to you, you know the drill."

"I know. No comment." It's been the same since I got hurt my first and only year in the pros. We got really good at *"no comment"* back then.

I silently nod. "None of it matters. The deal is happening. The organization included a house in my contract. Maybe you could help Kennedy pick out a few things for her new room this week."

Kennedy isn't a big fan of change. It makes her anxious. I'm hoping that being closer to Isla and Shaun will make things easier than they've been since they moved down to

Philadelphia from Boston. I haven't gotten nearly enough time with Kennedy this past year, and I can't even pretend that spending more time with my daughter isn't the best part of this new job opportunity.

"I actually wanted to talk to you about that, Deacon . . ." Isla trails off, and my body tightens, anticipating the hit coming my way, which years of knowing this woman has trained me to expect from that tone of voice.

I've been waiting for it since I told Shaun and her I wanted more time with Kennedy, now that I'll be closer.

Shaun is a VP at a Fortune 100 tech company outside of Philadelphia. Not exactly an easy drive for weekend visitation when I was coaching in Boston. Isla and I have spent Kennedy's life with a solid custody agreement in place, but it was one that didn't give me as much time with my daughter as I wanted. However, it was the best thing for her.

Isla was unusually quiet when I broke what I thought was exciting news about my new job and the move to Philly that came with it this weekend.

Isla is never quiet.

I should have been on high alert.

She stays quiet for another few moments before she blows out a heavy breath. "Listen, I'm sorry I didn't mention this when you were here, but in my defense, Shaun just got the final word after you'd already left."

"Final word on what?" I ask, cracking my neck left and right as the tension tightens my muscles.

"Shaun is being relocated," she sighs, and I freeze.

"Where?" I ask, not waiting for an answer before pushing harder. "Where is the transfer to, Isla?" An angry heat works its way down my body as my fist balls against the steering wheel.

"Japan," she answers, knowing the blow she's dealing.

"What the hell, Isla!" I yell loud enough inside my truck

THE SWEET SPOT

that the elderly couple who just walked into the parking lot stop and stare at me, probably checking to see if I'm about to murder someone.

"That's not just a transfer. That's a whole other fucking continent. You can't even take our daughter out of the country without my written consent. You sure as fuck can't just move her across the goddamned world and think I'm going to let you."

"You're upset—"

"You're fucking right, I'm upset," I yell before pressing down against my temples. "Half the reason I just took this job with the Revolution was to be closer to Kennedy, and now you're trying to take her away from me. I might not enforce it, Isla, but we have a fifty/fifty custody agreement. Don't forget it."

"Hey, you need to calm down and not threaten me, Deacon. I'm not the enemy here."

"Oh, I'm as calm as I'm getting, Isla. And if you're trying to take my daughter from me, that makes you *my* enemy." I stare at her name displayed on the Bluetooth screen and grind my teeth so hard I should be glad they don't crack.

This isn't the life I want for Kennedy.

"*Our* daughter," Isla corrects me. "And we'll figure this out. Together. Like we always do."

"If you try to take her out of this country, I will fight you with everything I have," I warn as calmly as I can.

"We'll talk more when we get home next weekend, Deacon. I'll send more pics. Go get some sleep and let me know how your meeting with the Kingstons goes tomorrow." She says the words like everything is fine, and she didn't just toss a grenade in my lap as she steps back to have a better view of its destruction.

"This. Isn't. Settled," I tell her before ending the call.

I've had to fight for every single thing in my life, and my

ex-wife is in for a world of pain if she thinks I'm going to roll over without fighting for my daughter.

Brynlee

My phone rings as I finish blow-drying my hair, fresh from the shower. I envy women who can wash their hair and go. If I let my hair air-dry, I'd look like a hot mess. My curls aren't the tight ringlets they were when I was younger, but those suckers are still making my life harder than it needs to be.

I flip my head over and run my fingers through the thick hair once before popping back up and looking at the phone with hesitation when I see it's my mother . . . *again*. This is the fourth time she's called today, and if I don't give in and answer her, she's just as likely to show up at my front door, calling my bluff.

Don't ever play poker with my mother. She'll call your bluff every time.

I slide my finger across the screen and hit the speaker option, then wait . . . because I can. Bratty, yes. But also effective.

"Brynlee St. James," her voice calls out to me. "I've been calling you all day."

Like there's any possible way I missed that.

"I've been busy, Mom." I grab tinted moisturizer and look at my reflection in the mirror, gently touching the dark circles under my eyes before I shake my head, exhausted. Fatigue sucks on a good day, and today may have started good, but damn, did it go downhill quickly. "I was going to call you back."

"Would that have been before your next birthday?" she asks with a sarcastic lilt to her frustrated voice.

"My birthday is four months away, Mom."

"Exactly," she counters. "I'd hoped to see you today. Killian came for dinner and said you were moving. What's he talking about?"

My little brother might be the prodigal son MMA fighter like our father, but I can and will kick his sorry ass the next time I see him.

Fuck this.

I stare at my reflection in the mirror as I draw in what feels like the final breath of strength I have left in my entire body. "I decided to trade condos with Maddox and Callen. I didn't need all that space, and the guys wanted the extra room to spread out. We spent most of today moving things around."

"Oh," she answers, and I think I have may have shocked my mother speechless for the first time in my life. "Well . . . I suppose that makes sense. Killian mentioned Maddox said there's extra room if he's still thinking about moving out. I hope you made them do all the heavy lifting. You don't need to be doing that, Brynn."

"I'm fine, Mom." Irritation clings to the thick air surrounding me. "If you already knew what happened, why did you ask?"

An alert pops up on my phone with a pinging notification. Apparently, the *Kroydon Kronicles* has gotten hold of the Revolution's deal with Deacon Kane. Not that I'm surprised. They seem to get everything before anyone else in this damn town, and more often than not, my friends and I seem to be at the center of their attention.

I've had alerts set for mention of the Revolution or Kings

teams in their columns for the past two years. I may also have my name and my friends' names all set for alerts too. I like to be prepared.

I wonder, briefly, if Deacon's seen this.

If he even knows about the *Kroydon Kronicles*.

If he's as tired as I am.

If his offer still stands.

My mind wanders to this morning. To the excitement that danced over my skin and tugged at something deeper . . . Room 210 . . . That's what he said earlier.

"Brynlee . . . are you listening to me?" my mother asks, letting her annoyance at being ignored sneak blatantly back in.

I'm about to answer when a quiet knock at the door makes me wonder if I'm hearing things. Until it's repeated again. That's definitely a knock.

"I've got to go, Mom. Someone's at the door."

"Brynlee . . . you're going to have to talk to me."

I pick the phone up, wishing I could go back to the sunrise from this morning. Back to the beach . . . back to the peace.

"I know, Mom. But I meant what I said earlier. Uncle Max will have my resignation on his desk first thing tomorrow morning. I'll stop by this week."

"Brynlee—"

"Gotta go, Mom. Bye." I disconnect the call and walk into my bedroom in my boy-cut panties and dark purple racerback tank top, then slide into a pair of jeans before walking down the hall to answer the door. A quick glance through the peephole probably should shock me, but it doesn't.

I swing the heavy door open and smile coyly at the tall, dark, and handsome hockey player standing before me. He's not the one I'd like to be looking at though. "Ares Wilder. What are you doing here?"

It's rhetorical.

I saw the way he's been looking at Grace this weekend.

I know that look.

He opens his mouth to answer, but I raise my hand, stopping him before he can speak. "No. Wait. Don't answer that." I step aside and let him in. "Let me go get Grace."

"Brynn . . ." he starts, but I shake my head.

"Nope. Stop. I don't want to know. This way I don't have to lie later." I take a few steps back. "You stay here."

He nods but follows my order the same way he would if he was coming to see me at work. Ares is a good guy. A good man, really. He just gets a bad rap from hanging out with the wrong people. He lets people assume the worst and never corrects them. But I see him, even if very few others have taken the time to look past the party boy headlines.

"For what it's worth, you'd be good for her."

Ares's ever-present grin slides into place. "I don't know what you're talking about, Doc."

It's my turn to smile. "Don't hurt my friend, god of war," I warn before turning down the hall.

Gracie's door is cracked open, and I knock once, then pop my head in. "Hey. I'm heading out."

She's lying on her bed in a white robe, her skin pink from the shower, looking as drained as I feel, but she manages to push herself up when she sees me. "You look pretty. Going somewhere fun?"

I walk over and tug her hair out of the messy bun on top of her head and fluff it around her shoulders.

"What the hell?" Grace laughs as she smacks my hands away.

I quirk a brow and purse my lips to hold back my laugh. "Don't ask me where I'm going, and I won't ask you why Ares is standing in our new living room," I offer her as a truce instead.

"What?" She pops up to her feet, straightening her robe and giving me her complete attention now with that new small nugget of information. Grace's eyes grow wide before settling into their own deviousness. "Wait . . . so you're going to see a man?" Gracie may be the quiet twin, but she's certainly not a stupid twin. Neither she nor Everly could ever be called that.

The thing is, I'm not ready to talk just yet.

Instead, I shake my head and place my pointer finger in front of my lips. "See you bright and early tomorrow for your evaluation, good twin."

I walk away, smiling.

If all goes well tonight, maybe it won't exactly be bright and early . . .

BRYNLEE

Some girls grew up wanting to be the princess saved from the dragon by the handsome prince. I wanted to be the dragon slayer. Now . . . I want to be the dragon rider. I guess I can thank romance books for that evolution.

—Brynlee's Secret Thoughts

Fifteen minutes later, I find myself listening to the last chapter of the epic fantasy romance I'm currently binging on Audible. And okay, so maybe . . . just maybe, I'm using it as a stalling tactic while I sit parked in front of the Kroydon Hills Plaza Hotel. The last few words of the book play out on my Bluetooth before I wipe an errant tear from my cheek. *Damn it.* I swear I always cry when I've invested so much time in a series, and the hero and heroine finally get their happily ever after.

I grew up watching the most modern fairytale imaginable play out between my parents.

Their love was tangible.

It had its own heartbeat.

My father encouraged my mother to be the strongest woman in any room but never let her forget he was always going to be there, standing next to her, holding her hand, and giving her his strength when she needed it.

Scarlet Kingston was the original dragon rider in my eyes.

You'd think that would make me a daydreamer, desperate for her chance at the kind of love I grew up watching. And maybe I was at some point. But life seems to have other plans for me.

Plans that might not look the way I thought they would.

Plans that I'm still trying to come to terms with.

As the credits roll on my book, I push the button to turn off my car and silently count to ten, giving myself an out.

Right now, Deacon Kane doesn't know I'm here.

We haven't crossed any weird work lines, and we don't owe each other a single thing.

That all changes if I go upstairs.

Which leads me to ask myself, *again*, what the hell I'm doing here.

Room 210... His husky voice whispers in my ear as if he's standing right next to me, his hot breath tickling my sensitive skin, instead of being an already distant memory more than twelve hours after leaving him on the beach. No sooner does that thought trickle in and out of my mind than I'm closing the car door behind me with anticipation thrumming through my veins for the first time in a long time. A smile plays on my lips because I know exactly why I drove here.

I did it for myself.

I felt more alive lying in the cold sand next to Deacon than I'd felt in months, and I. Want. More.

More sparks.

More life.

Just. More. Time.

With steadier feet than I'd expect to have, I walk by the front desk and wave at the woman standing behind it, her face familiar from classes I teach at Crucible. I don't stop to chat, eager to garner as little attention as possible. It's been months since I was the focus of a *Kroydon Kronicles* article, and I'd like to keep it that way for as long as possible.

The fewer people who see me here, the better.

I slip quietly onto the elevator and press the button for the second floor, then wait for an eternity to pass before the doors finally close. No sooner have I exhaled the breath I was unknowingly holding than the doors open once more, and I'm left scanning the hall for prying eyes before taking a few steps toward one of the first doors and raising hesitant knuckles to knock on the door of Room 210.

My hand hangs in the air, fisted and frozen as my emotions go to war.

Can something be equally stupid and out of character and yet completely worth it at the same time?

Guess I'm about to find out.

I've barely touched the door when it's swung open, and I'm met with Deacon standing just inside. A white towel is knotted at his hips as water droplets run down from his jet-black hair. A sexy smirk slides into place when any words I may have prepared die a quick death on my suddenly dry lips.

Ho-ly hell. This man is just so . . . *much.*

Broad, beautifully carved shoulders slope down to a chest I'd love to get my hands on, strictly in a professional manner . . . of course. His pecs are pure perfection, and as a few lucky droplets of water sluice over beautiful, tanned washboard abs—I manage to count eight . . . *Eight.*

This man is the epitome of a golden god, and I may have

just swallowed my own tongue because I stand here without words, fighting to shake myself out of whatever trance I seem to be frozen in.

"St. James." My name sounds more like a curse than a greeting from his lips. "Didn't think you were coming."

He doesn't step aside or ask me in, and suddenly I find myself wondering if I read him and the entire situation wrong. The backs of my eyelids burn with embarrassment, and I have no doubt a crimson red wave of heat is washing over my face.

Seriously? The first time I put myself out there in forever, this is what happens?

Screw this and screw him for making me feel this way.

"You know what?" I shake my head, aggravated that I've allowed myself to be so vulnerable. "I shouldn't have come. I've had a bad day, and I guess I wasn't thinking straight. It won't happen again."

"That's it? Didn't know you'd give up so easily," he challenges, and I taste the coppery tang of blood in my mouth as I bite down on my bottom lip to keep my smart mouth in check.

I'm going to have to work with this man, if only for the next month.

It's still a damn month.

"Give up?" I counter, getting ready to go toe-to-toe, but Deacon looks up toward the ceiling for a hot second before bringing his stormy blue gaze back to mine. And when he does, I don't see a man ready to spar. *That* I know how to deal with. I've been doing it for years in every aspect of my life. No . . . this man looks wrecked.

"I'm sorry. That's not what I fucking meant. Guess you're not the only one who's had a bad day." He runs his fingers through his hair, moving it off his face. The action draws me back to that beautiful body and the way it moves. I'd love to study this man's muscles. *Again . . . in a purely professional way.* "I thought you were room service. I've got a pizza and beer coming up. Want to share shit-day stories over dinner?" He pushes the door wider and steps aside. "You gonna come in or make me stand here in a towel until somebody snaps a picture they can sell to the tabloids?"

Guess he did see the *Kroydon Kronicles* article after all.

Better get used to it in this town.

I walk by him with a roll of my eyes. "Not sure anyone would buy that picture, Kane. We've got a lot of athletes in Kroydon Hills, and they've been caught in less,"—I drag my eyes over his chest with a smile and tease—"and looking better."

Deacon

This spitfire walks by me like she owns the hotel, and for all I know—*or care*—she might. Her bare arm brushes mine, and my hair stands on end. This woman . . . *Damn*, I'm glad she's not looking at me because something about her less than impressed attitude and the insane fucking electricity thrashing between us like a live wire makes it hard to hide my cock jumping to attention behind my towel. My eyes stay locked on her as the streetlights filtering in through the curtains bathe her in a warm glow.

"Give me a minute," I groan before grabbing sweats and making my way into the bathroom. I throw them on, then pick up the t-shirt I tossed on the floor earlier and sniff.

Yeah . . . that's not gonna work.

When I step back into the bedroom, Brynlee's thanking the room service guy. She turns to me with a sexy smile on her face and pizza and beer in each of her hands, having no idea that standing in front of me the way she is right now, she's my fucking dream girl. No makeup. A tight tank top and a pair of jeans with holes in both knees. She radiates comfort and confidence, and *fuck,* that's sexy. Add the pizza and beer, and I'd have to beat men off with a hockey stick if they were lucky enough to see what I'm seeing. And I'd do it willingly for this woman.

I don't share.

"You better get a shirt on, Kane. Wouldn't want to drip any grease on that pretty chest. You've got to look good for the front page of the tabloids, after all." Her smile stretches across her beautiful face and lights up those green eyes, and I know, without a shadow of a doubt, I'm a goner.

Brynlee places the food on the table and pulls a beer bottle out of the six pack. She inspects it with a perfectly arched eyebrow. "Good choice. This is my cousin's beer."

I grab an old Boston University tee from the edge of the bed before I take the beer she's holding out for me. "Oh yeah? I figured I'd try the local IPA."

She twists the cap off and steps back, watching me with careful eyes. "Go ahead. I want to know if you like it."

"Awfully invested in your cousin's beer, St. James. You guys must be close."

Her face drops before she scowls. "The asshole took my condo today. So I'm not really sure how to answer that." She searches through the brown bag on top of the pizza box and pulls out paper plates and napkins. Then she puts them on the table before placing the remainder of the six pack in the fridge, while she helps herself to a bottle of water before sitting down. She looks up at me with pursed lips and a sparkle in her eyes. "Are you going to sit to eat, or do you expect me to cut your pizza too?" she teases with a laugh, and fuck . . . I like her sass.

I drop down onto the chair and tear away a slice, then push the plate in front of her before serving myself. She might be feeling salty tonight, but I do have manners. Even if the eating I'd like to do right now doesn't involve pizza or a plate. I watch her fold the pizza in half and wait for the grease to drip off before she takes a bite, and I'm pretty fucking sure I've never been jealous of a slice of pizza before right now.

We eat in silence, both of us lost in our own thoughts for a minute until Brynlee cracks open her water bottle and catches me staring. "So . . . why was your day such a shit show?"

I shake my head no. "Uh-uh. My momma taught me manners. Ladies always come first."

Her breath catches on a silent gasp, and I know she's feeling this crazy connection too before she quickly recovers. Her shoulders rise with a deep inhale before she blows out a breath. "Let's see . . . I made a stupid bet with my cousin because I trusted my mother. A mistake I had to learn the hard way. Because, thanks to her, I lost the bet and my job."

"What the hell? Your job with the Revolution?"

What kind of fucked up family is the Kingstons?

"I didn't lose my job so much as quit." She takes another bite of the pizza, and I can't take my eyes off her.

Could she possibly have any clue what she's doing to me or the hold she already has on me? When I don't say anything, she finally answers my silent question. "My mother wanted to move me over to work with the Philadelphia Kings football team. Which would mean working under her instead of Max."

"And that would be bad?" I ask without thinking it

through, and the look Brynlee gives me would cut a lesser man down. Good thing I'm not a lesser man.

"My mother and I . . ." she chews her lip. "We wouldn't work well together. We'd probably kill each other in the process. But it's not even that. I worked hard to get where I am, and I love this team. I never wanted to work with the football team. I always knew the only other place I'd love as much as the Revolution would be working for Crucible."

"Your dad's gym?" It's a rhetorical question. Crucible is well-known to anyone who's ever followed MMA.

The anger disappears from her face, and a gorgeous smile appears in its place as she nods. "I grew up in that place. The octagon was my playground. The fighters were my first babysitters. If it wasn't hockey players, it was always going to be fighters. So I quit. I gave my mom thirty days' notice, and tomorrow, I'll tell my dad I'm finally ready to take him up on his offer."

She shrugs, like quitting her job is no big deal, and I'm reminded of what different lives we've led. Quitting a job without having another lined up has never been an option in my life.

"And you're sure your dad will hire you?" I ask, as interested in her answer as I am in the sound of her voice.

She nods and rips the crust from her pizza, then points it at me like she's waving a wand.

"Hey, now, Hermione. Don't point that thing at me."

Her face softens, and her smile spreads, deviously. "Are you a Potterhead, Deacon?"

"Kennedy and I have been reading chapters together at night over FaceTime. It was a great way to get to spend time with her, even if we were in different states." I lean back in my chair and sip my beer, ignoring the anger that bubbles right under the surface when I think about Isla wanting to take my daughter across the world. "We're up to *The Prisoner of Azkaban.*"

"That's sweet. I bet she's a real daddy's girl."

"Yeah. But her stepdad just got offered a promotion that would move them to Japan, and I hate the idea of being a FaceTime father for the next two years. Not sure how that's gonna work yet," I groan through gritted teeth.

"Oh, Deacon. I'm so sorry." She reaches her hand across the table and rests it on my forearm, and even through my frustration, her touch heats my skin. "What are you going to do?"

"No fucking clue," I admit, so fucking frustrated that just when I thought I'd get to have my daughter in my life more than FaceTimes and summers, she's going to be ripped even further away than she is now.

Brynlee pops up from the table and clears our plates with a smile, then turns to me. "Come on, Kane. Get up."

"What are you thinking, crazy girl?" I ask with a gruff laugh.

She holds her hand out for me. "What? Are you scared?"

I take her hand in mine and stand, then lift my other hand to her face. "Of you? Not hardly, Brynn."

She licks her lips as her green eyes darken to a shade you only see in pictures of the Irish countryside. "Maybe you should be," she whispers, and fuck . . . maybe she's right.

BRYNLEE

"Where the hell are we going, red?" A chill skirts down my spine, which I absolutely refuse to acknowledge. At least not yet. But that one word does things to my body that no word should be able to do. Even though I'm completely aware that it's this man with that mouth speaking that word—that's the lethal combination.

"We're almost there," I placate and tug him along behind me, ducking through the monstrously tall evergreen trees that create a thick privacy fence at the edge of the property line shared with old Mrs. Golden.

I stop at the edge of the lake and turn to face the giant of a man behind me, loosening my fingers that are laced with Deacon's to tug them free. But he tightens his grip on mine, refusing to break the connection. "Is trespassing your idea of a good time?" Deacon asks with a mischievous glint in his eye.

With a worn Boston University t-shirt and baseball cap pulled low over his eyes, this man might not be easily recognizable in this town yet. But he soon will be. His face will be well-known. His moves documented like the rest of the professional athletes who choose to live in this typically sleepy little suburb of Philadelphia. But for tonight, I get to keep him to myself, and I can admit that gives me a little thrill.

"Can it really be trespassing if my family owns the property, and they're giving it to you in a contract tomorrow?" I tease, attempting again to pull away, but his grip is unfaltering on my hand. "I'm not going to run away. You can let go of my hand now."

I kick off my flip flops, then look down at his sneakers. "Take your shoes off."

"Why?" he asks, even as he steps out of them while I smile triumphantly.

"Because studies show standing in the grass grounds you. It can relieve stress and negativity and can help you sleep better." I scrunch my toes into the damp earth beneath my feet, then take a few steps back, pulling on Deacon's hold. "I figured we could both use a little stress relief."

"Oh yeah?" With one step and a tug of his hand, he closes the distance between us, leaving barely a breath separating us. Electricity sizzles and snaps, this crazy connection growing stronger with each new touch. Deacon's smile is slow and so damn sexy. "You need help relieving your stress, Brynn?"

Deacon's free hand slides around the back of my neck. His thumb caresses the column of my throat, and I melt. My panties dampen, and my breath catches in my chest as I gently nod, whispering, hoarsely, "I could use some help."

He drops his other hand, cups my face, and bends his knees, bringing us eye to eye. "Tell me what you need."

Good lord.

His low, gravelly, growly voice is my undoing.

With a push of my hand against his muscled chest, I'm finally able to step back. My gaze locks with Deacon's, and I slowly pull my tank over my head, enjoying the flames growing in his heated gaze that's reflected back at me. I drop my shirt to the ground, then hook my thumbs in my jeans and shimmy them over my hips and down my legs.

I watch his Adam's apple work as Deacon silently swallows.

Nerves war with need, and my lips tremble with anticipation when I finally answer him, "I need you to make sure I don't drown, Kane."

His eyes flare for a moment frozen in time I'll never forget before I take off for the safety of the lake. One I'm in no danger of drowning in. I've swam in this lake my entire life, racing my cousins to see who could make it to the falls on the other side fastest.

I take off for the dock, and the loud pounding of my heart nearly silences the sounds of Deacon undressing behind me. Before I can catapult myself into the cold water, the sound of heavy footfalls gains on me. I'm lifted in strong arms and cradled against a hard chest before we both crash into the abyss below.

Deacon

The dark lake crashes over us as I kick back up to the surface, refusing to let go of Brynlee. She feels right in my arms. Like she's meant to be there. Her words play again in my mind.

Make sure I don't drown.

She spits water out as we surface, and the sheer white lace

of her bra does nothing to hide the most magnificent breasts I've ever fucking seen as they press against my bare chest.

Make sure I don't drown.

"What the fuck were you thinking?" I growl, while an unfamiliar feeling tugs deep in my chest.

Brynlee turns in my hold, wrapping her arms around my neck. I slide one arm down to cup her ass and one hand up to the back of her head. We bob in the water until I'm able to move us up against the dock, where my feet touch the sand below.

Water droplets cling to her long dark lashes as she flutters them up at me, the freckles dotting the bridge of her nose barely visible as her skin practically glows in the moonlight. "I thought a midnight swim could be fun," she says softly, a new hesitance in her voice, one I haven't heard yet, but want to learn.

Fuck.

I want to learn everything there is to know about this woman.

"You thought it could be *fun*?" I ask, so fucking far gone, I can't control the tone of my voice. She's driving me insane. Her legs shift against my ragingly hard dick that missed the message that cold water was supposed to slow the blood flow down. I'm hard as hell and pressing against my boxer briefs, while the infuriating woman in my arms smiles like a little redheaded nymph. "Drowning sounds like fun to you?"

With a soft laugh, she pushes my hair away from my face. "I can swim, Deacon. I was captain of the swim team in high school."

My grip on her ass tightens, and she wraps her legs around my hips with another hum while her teeth sink into her pouty pink lip.

"Brynlee," I murmur as I run my nose up her neck, one

hand sliding under her lace panties and over her perfect bare ass cheek.

Her head drops back against the dock on a sweet sigh, and her nails dig into the hair at the nape of my neck. She rocks her hips against my hard cock, and a soft sound slips past her trembling lips.

"You better be sure you want this, red. Because I don't fucking share," I warn before our lips crash together in answer.

She tastes like sweetness wrapped in sin.

She *tastes* like mine.

The fucking Earth tilts on its axis, and the world around us ceases to exist. I capture her mouth with mine, sliding my tongue against hers, savoring the taste of her, and swallowing her beautiful moan while she fucking clings to me. Long nails scratch my scalp and dig into my hair. My tongue pushes against hers as I lean her back against the dock's wooden pylon, freeing my hand so I can learn the curves of her body. The dip of her hips, the flat plane of her stomach. I cup her breast in my hand, and she mewls against my mouth until I push her bra up and rip it in half, shoving it off her.

"Deacon," she gasps against my lips as her body clings to me.

"I'll buy you another one," I growl against her mouth, then take one perfectly pink-tipped breast into my mouth.

"Oh God."

She grabs my face in her hands and yanks me back to her lips, then presses down against my cock, and there's no mistaking the need in our frenzy.

My fingers slide inside her panties and over her bare pussy. I dip one inside her tight core, and the beautiful fucking sound she makes is my undoing.

She bites at my lip and grinds against me.

"I don't have a condom, red. It's in my wallet somewhere on the fucking grass."

"Fuck the condom," she pants. "I've got an IUD."

Possession roars through my blood, and I add a second finger while I drag my teeth over her throat as I get her ready for me. "Be sure, red," I warn her again, circling her clit, then plunging my fingers back in. When she moans and claws at my back, I pull them back out. "Words, Brynlee. I need your words."

Her glittering green eyes light with a surprising tease before she kisses me slowly, tracing my bottom lip with her tongue before her teeth graze over it. "Deacon . . ." she whispers, then kisses me again. Her tongue presses into my mouth, tangling with mine. Driving me fucking crazy. "Please . . ." she pleads. "Please. Please. Please . . . fuck me."

She peppers kisses along my jaw.

"Make me scream," she whispers against my skin, and the tight grip I've got on my sanity cracks.

She drags her tongue along my earlobe, then bites down before softening the sting with her tongue.

"Make me come," she commands me, like a queen commanding a servant.

My fucking queen.

BRYNLEE

The stars light up the dark summer sky and reflect off the even darker water, bathing us both in a silvery, ethereal glow. I trail my fingers along Deacon's strong shoulders as he drags the thick head of his cock through my core. Goosebumps break out over my heated skin as the cool water laps at us.

It's all too much, and yet not nearly enough.

"Deacon . . ." I whisper with bated breath, desperate . . . needy.

For this . . . For *him*.

The gentle crashing of the waterfalls behind us works in unison with the shadow of the dock to keep us in darkness, hidden in our own world.

Deacon's hand wraps around the back of my head, his thumb caressing my jaw as he stares at me. "You are so fucking pretty, Brynn."

His words are growled against my skin as he slides himself through my sex.

Watching my every breath. Pushing in the tiniest bit before pulling out again.

Teasing me until I tug his hair, ready to scream.

But before I can find words, callused fingers grip my jaw, holding me still. His thumb presses against my lower lip before he covers my mouth with his. Firm lips own me as I surrender to him. Each wicked stroke of his tongue takes me higher until I'm teetering on the edge of lucidity, unsure how much more I can take. My body is strung tight like a bow ready to snap until he finally pushes his cock inside me—filling me to the point of pain, overwhelming my senses until I can't focus on anything but this moment and this man—and I gasp. Agony and ecstasy fight for control while I feel like I'm being ripped in half in the most sinfully decadent way I've ever imagined.

"Deacon, oh God," I cry out against his lips.

"Fuck . . . Brynn. Your pretty cunt is taking my cock like such a good girl." He worships me with his mouth, whispering filthy words that stoke the already-building inferno within me.

With each achingly slow stroke of his cock, my muscles contract around him.

Stretching to take him deeper. Clawing to get closer.

And when he finally fills me completely, my body explodes. Every nerve catches fire. Lighting up like the sky on the Fourth of July.

I'm utterly consumed by him.

"Deacon . . ."

His tongue slips down the length of my throat, sucking on my thrumming pulse. "Tell me how it feels, baby."

His head dips back down to take my aching nipple in his mouth, and I gasp, "So fucking good."

"Fuck, Brynlee." He pulls out slowly, then sets a punishing rhythm with every hard snap of his hips. His big body dominates mine, all hard planes pressing decadently against soft curves in the most delicious ways.

I tighten my legs around his hips as the water sloshes between us, and I take everything he gives me.

Deacon's foot slips, and he wraps both arms around me, moving us away from the dock.

Fucking me harder and harder.

Fanning the flames higher and higher until I'm completely overwhelmed.

Destroying me.

"So close," I whisper as I drop my head to his neck and suck his salty, sweet skin.

The connection between us is more intense than anything I've ever imagined.

"You gonna come on my cock, Brynn?" he growls. *Actually growls*. And I moan incoherently as if his words were what I was waiting for, and my orgasm is ripped from my body.

Deacon's lips capture mine, swallowing my screams as my entire body vibrates, and my walls clamp down on his cock. Tears leak from the corner of my eyes as warmth washes over me, and he fills me completely, coming with my name on his lips like a sacred prayer.

Breaking me in ways I never knew possible and may never recover from.

He holds me against him until a chill skirts down my skin.

"Shit, red. We don't even have towels."

I lift my face to his, unable to comprehend the look in his eyes.

It's guilt. But why?

"Deacon—" I start before he cuts me off.

"Damn it. I shouldn't have—"

"Don't you dare." I place a gentle finger over his lips as he bends his knees and drops us both under the water. "Don't even think about finishing that sentence."

I ghost my lips over his. "A little water never hurt anyone."

An incredibly sexy smile spreads over his handsome face. "Where the hell have you been all my life?"

He cups my face, and I lean my cheek into his hand. "Right here, waiting for you to notice me."

Deacon laughs and presses his lips to my forehead. "Pretty sure you've never gone for lack of notice, Brynlee."

I close my eyes and soak it all in.

The moon . . . The stars . . . The night . . . *The man.*

Sometime after the sun has already risen, I lay naked and splayed across Deacon's chest, having traded in the lake for a king-sized bed with 1500 thread count sheets. Neither of us has slept a wink . . . again, and Deacon's hand is making its hundredth pass up and down my spine when I rest my chin on his chest and tilt my face to his. "What are you going to do?"

"About what?" he murmurs in a rough, sleep-deprived voice, exhaustion catching up with both of us.

"Kennedy," I answer softly and trace the tip of my finger over his pec. "Is there anything I can do to help?"

"I don't know. I'm not sure what I *can* do, yet." He looks over at the clock on the nightstand and groans. "I'm meeting with management at nine to sign my contract. I guess I'll figure Isla out after that."

"Oh yeah?" I drag out and press my lips to his chest. "I'll be there with Gracie tomorrow."

"Gracie?" he asks as he flips me over to my back and presses his lips to my collarbone.

I hold his face in my hands and enjoy the calm before the storm. "Grace Sinclair. She's one of my best friends. We all lived together in college and for a while after college. Gracie is a ballerina in London, but she's hurt, and she's home, staying with me while I help her rehab."

Deacon kisses his way down my chest and over my stomach, then stops and stares when my body revolts from the lack of food I had yesterday, growling so loudly, he's probably scared an alien is about to break free.

"Oh my God." I bury my face in my hands, and Deacon hops up from the bed. "What are you doing?" I ask, mortified.

"Ordering breakfast. I plan to keep you busy for at least another hour, so you're going to need some carbs. Waffles sound good?"

He looks at me as he lifts the phone, and I nod, not used to being taken care of.

I tend to be the caretaker.

"Yes, this is Deacon Kane in 210. I'd like to order Belgium waffles with whipped cream." He looks at me as he stands there, naked and oh, so impressive. "We're going to need extra whipped cream. And can you bring a plate of cherries and a bowl of oatmeal with a banana." He covers the phone with his hand. "Anything else?"

"Coffee," I tell him.

"Yes, and two cups of coffee and a carafe of orange juice. Twenty minutes. Got it. Thanks." He hangs up, then leans down and throws me over his shoulder like he's throwing around a ten-pound bag of potatoes instead of an actual person. Deacon smacks my bare ass as he walks us into the bathroom, and I've gotta say, I've never been manhandled before, but holy hell, it's hot.

He sits me on the counter and turns the warm water on, adjusting the temperature until he's satisfied, then scoops me back up. "Oh my God, Deacon. I can walk," I giggle as he walks us both into the massive shower.

Have I mentioned how much I love this hotel?

Because right about now, as the two showerheads rain down over us and this man gently sets me on my feet, I'm fairly certain this steam shower may have just surpassed the luxury sheets in the *what I'm grateful for* department.

However, that all fades to black as Deacon drops to his knees and drapes one of my legs over his shoulder.

I leave Deacon in the shower to wash his hair and grab one of the fluffy robes hanging from the bathroom door and don't even bother to check out what kind of hot mess I must look like before I run to the door. "I'm coming," I call out right before I open the door, expecting room service. Only instead of a friendly hotel employee greeting me, an incredibly beautiful woman with shiny, short dark hair stands across from me with a questioning look.

"Oh," she laughs. "I didn't know Deacon had company." She walks right by me like I invited her in, and I'm left staring at her like I should know who she is.

I close the door and tie my robe a little tighter, my fight-or-flight instinct starting to kick in, leaving me unsure which instinct is currently winning.

"I'm so sorry. Where are my manners? I'm Isla. It's wonderful to meet you. Deacon didn't tell me he was seeing someone. This is great news."

I stand there silent, having no clue what I'm supposed to

say when another knock on the door comes, followed by Deacon's voice. "I'll be right out, red."

"You might want to hurry," I yell back as I open the door. Blessedly, this time, it *is* room service. "Thanks," I tell him and let him wheel the little cart in, happy for any distraction from the strange smiling ex-wife, who's standing on the other side of the room that's growing smaller by the minute.

What the fuck is she smiling about?

I don't do *extrovert* in the morning before I've had at least one strong cup of coffee.

Deacon walks out of the bathroom the same way he opened the door for me last night, though now I know from personal inspection exactly what he's hiding behind that towel. He ignores the food and stalks toward me instead, wrapping a hand around my head before I press both palms against his chest, stopping him.

"You, okay?" he asks, confused, and I nod toward Isla, who looks like she's about to start clapping any minute.

"Hi." She waves at Deacon, and I swear this woman is way too happy for this early in the morning.

Happy, peaceful Deacon, who spent an entire night worshipping my body, disappears in one single heartbeat. His brows pull tight, and his body tenses. "Is Kennedy okay?"

"Of course. She's fine. I would have called you if she wasn't," Isla assures him before glancing back to me.

"What are you doing here?" he asks, but her focus stays solely on me. "I thought you were staying at the beach through Friday."

"You know what? I should go." I turn, but Deacon grabs the robe's sash and tugs.

"Stay," he says softly. And I consider it for a moment.

"Yes, stay. If you're in Deacon's life, then you're in Kennedy's life, and I should get to know you." Isla tells me, before she finally does it.

She actually claps her hands together once, then clasps them in front of herself.

I look from him to her with an almost unbearable nervous energy and fight the urge to say *peace out*. Because I'm for sure, peacing the fuck out of this situation. One night, with absolutely no promises or any discussions of where we stand, because—*hello, it was one night*—doesn't mean I need to be involved in a conversation between Deacon and the mother of his child slash ex-wife, who's probably spent hundreds of hours worshipping the body I was just—

Okay. Time to cut off that train of thought. *STAT*.

"This sounds like a conversation better had between the two of you." I tug the sash away from him and watch as disappointment spreads over his chiseled face. *I'll see you later*, I mouth silently before grabbing my clothes and changing in the bathroom.

This just became the strangest walk of shame I've ever done.

Deacon

My ex-wife sits primly on the couch, apparently much more well rested than I am, staring at me as I watch the hotel room door shut with a deafening click behind the woman who just blew my fucking mind.

"Holy shit, Deacon Kane. That woman's got you bad. Deacon, the bachelor, is done. I can see it in your eyes."

I open my mouth to stop her, but Isla steamrolls over me like she always does. "I can't even tell you how happy that makes me. I mean, it changes things . . . sort of." She hops up on her white sandals, beaming like I just handed her the world, and I'm not really following.

A night of non-stop mind-blowing sex and no sleep will definitely slow response time.

I may have left my higher-level reasoning in that lake.

I smirk to myself ... Or maybe it's on the shower floor.

"Deacon ... Are you listening to me?"

I cross my arms over my chest and shake my head. "We're divorced, Isla. I don't have to listen to you anymore. That's Shaun's job now."

She rolls her eyes the exact same way Kennedy does, and it makes me smile until I remember yesterday's call. "What are you doing here, Isla?"

"Shaun and I talked last night, and as much as the thought absolutely kills me, I think Kennedy should stay with you. We'll be gone a minimum of one year, but it could possibly be two. I don't think dragging our already-anxious daughter to a country where she doesn't know the language or the customs is fair to her. But I owe this to my husband. He's been working toward this position for years and already turned it down once before because he didn't want to put me in this position. He told me again last night that we don't have to do this, but he's lying to himself. He has to do this. If they pass him over again, he'll never get another chance. I'll try to come home as much as I can, but I don't know how often that will be."

I lean back against the dresser, unsure what I'm supposed to say.

"Isla ..."

"Don't, Deacon. I cried so much last night, I shouldn't have any tears left to cry. But they're right there, sitting behind my eyes, waiting for me to crack. It's why I forced Shaun to come home early. I needed to talk to you face-to-face. And I can't even tell you how happy I am to know that you have someone in your life. Will she be able to help you when you're on the road?"

She asks the question with so much hope that I take the coward's way out and nod.

I hadn't given that any thought because I took the job before Isla told me they were moving, and until now, I had no idea I'd become her primary parent.

I don't bother telling her I'm not sure what Brynlee and I are because I know what I want us to be. "She works for the hockey team now."

"Oh? In the office?" She stands and pours herself a cup of coffee, then adds a spoonful of whipped cream.

Fuck. I had plans for that whipped cream.

"No. She's the team's physical therapist. But she just gave her notice. Her father is a former MMA world champion. He runs a gym now, and she's going to work for him."

She crinkles her brow. "Was that . . . Are you in love with a Kingston?" She gasps, excitedly, and I groan in frustration.

"Boundaries, Isla."

"Fine. But that's her, right? Her mom runs the football team? The *Kroydon Kronicles* loves to write about her and her friends."

"Isla—"

"Deacon . . ."

"She's a St. James," I tell her even though Brynlee is every bit Kingston, even if it's not her last name.

She mimes zipping her lips.

"Do you need to figure out whether you can do this, Deacon? We're talking about our baby. If you're not sure whether you're up to it—"

"I don't need time. I'm her father, and this is what's best for our daughter. Thank you for trusting me, Isla." Her lip quivers, and she puts down her coffee and walks into my arms. We hug like the friends we are until she starts laughing and steps away.

"Two things."

I wait, not knowing where she's going with this.

"One, I want to do a dinner this weekend with all of us and your new Kingston."

"Her name is Brynlee . . ." I tell her and watch her smile at me. Sometimes I wonder how we ever thought getting married for the sake of her being pregnant was a good idea. We were always better as friends.

"Fine. I want to do dinner with Brynlee so I can see Kennedy and her together."

"I'm going back up to Boston later today. Dinner has to wait until I come back. Do you know when you're leaving for Japan?" I ask, not sure I'm ready for her answer.

"They want us there in a month, but I think Shaun pushed back for two months. I think they're going to meet somewhere in the middle with five or six weeks." She picks up her purse and points it at me. "Now put on some damn clothes. This whole McSteamy thing you've got going on is a bit much, Deacon." She kisses my cheek and crosses the room. "Let me know when you figure out when you'll be back, I want to do dinner, Deacon. I want to see our daughter meet your woman. And, let me know if you need help with Kennedy's room."

She walks over to the door and turns with her hand on the knob. "She's going to have to stay with you for a bit before the official move. We'll need to get her comfortable with it before it actually happens," she tells me, but it almost feels like a mental checklist she's going through for herself.

"Isla . . ." I call out until she finally stops and looks at me. "I mean it. Thank you."

"You're a good father, Deacon. And I'm a good mother. This is what's best for Kennedy. But you better get really good at FaceTime and have a spare room for me. Because I plan on flying home as much as I can. I've never been apart from her for more than the month you get her each summer, and I don't know how I'm going to do it."

I shake my head, and she laughs. "Tell Brynlee I'm sorry for interrupting whatever I interrupted this morning."

"Yeah. I probably won't be mentioning that."

She shrugs and walks out, and I'm left standing in the middle of this hotel room, wondering how my world just tilted on its axis for the second time in twelve hours.

DEACON

I'm waiting to be escorted into Max Kingston's office later that morning when Brynlee walks out of it and directly into my chest. My hands grip her shoulders momentarily before dropping, and she mumbles, "Excuse me," then hurries by without looking back.

Shit. I guess she just gave her official letter of resignation. She'd mentioned she was planning on doing that this morning.

I'm in crisis mode, running on no sleep. And as if that wasn't enough, my little hit-and-run, who just scurried away, has taken up all the extra space in my brain. I'm definitely regretting not trying to catch a few minutes of shut-eye after Isla left and hoping my reflexes are sharp enough to go toe-to-toe with the powerhouses in this room.

Max sits opposite me behind a massive desk. His reputation precedes him in every circle he's known. This man has helped take the sport of hockey to a new level and put this team in the rarefied air of the greats before them. His sister stands next to him, just as formidable, having run the Philadelphia Kings at an equally high level. With her arms crossed over her chest, she's looking at me like she's less than impressed. And that's without knowing all the ways I defiled her daughter last night.

I fight the smile pulling at my lips as I remember the look on Brynlee's face the first time she came and start mentally counting the hours until I can make her do it again.

These siblings run one of the most profitable companies to ever own one sports franchise, let alone two. And even though we've already done the interview, negotiated terms, and offered and accepted the position, I'm still half expecting them to tell me this is all one big joke. That they've judged me and found me lacking in some way and are rescinding their offer. Because hiring someone *my* age for *this* job is nearly unheard of.

The fact their family has been staying at my parents' inn each summer since I was playing pond hockey in peewees make it all the more difficult to believe.

"Thanks for coming in, Deacon." Max motions to the chair across from him. "Have a seat."

"Thank you," I respond as I sit, my eyes pulling to his massive windows that open to the rink below. Pristine ice gleams with the red, white, and blue Revolution logo proudly taking up residence at center ice.

"We've got Hunter conferenced in." Scarlet motions toward the phone.

"Yes, you do, and at an ungodly hour too, might I add," my agent answers, always unhappy with meetings that take place before noon.

"Listen, Hunter, this should be fast and painless," Max tells him as Scarlet scowls at her brother.

"Don't kiss his ass. You make enough money off our players, combined, to send your grandkids' grandkids to private boarding schools on our dime, Hunter." Her smile is calculated and cool as she picks up papers from Max's desk. "A nine a.m. meeting won't kill you."

Max and I are each handed a copy of the contract we've already agreed to. "Were there any questions or concerns with the contract?" she asks, looking over Max's shoulder.

"No. Everything looks good on our end," Hunter answers as I skim over the highlights again. It's all there. The salary. The bonuses. The expectations from both parties.

"Us too," Max agrees and signs his copy before handing it to Scarlet to do the same. Once she's done, I sign as well and try to act like I'm not a kid whose dream just came true. I hand the contract back to Max, who exchanges it for a manilla envelope.

"A copy of the press release that's going out later this week is in there, as well as the keys to the house and your contact for the relocation."

"Thank you for the opportunity," I tell them both as my mind races. "I have some loose ends I need to tie up in Boston over the next month. But I'm looking forward to working with you. On a personal note, my daughter is going to be coming to live with me full-time. I was wondering if there is anyone on staff who could possibly help me get her transferred into . . . Well, I guess I need to decide on a school first before I get her transferred."

Max pulls a card from his desk drawer. "My wife, Daphne, sits on the board of Kroydon Hills Prep. They're a K–12 school." He looks at his sister and smiles. "All our kids have gone through there. Scarlet and I went there back in the day too. It's a great school. If you want to give Daphne a call, I'm sure she'd be happy to help."

I stand and shake his hand. "Thanks, Max. I appreciate it."

"Listen, Deacon. I've been the new guy, and I've been the young guy, but that never stopped me from being the *right* guy. There's going to be a lot of talk about your age. Ignore it. We believe in you and what you're going to bring to the Revolution. You're our first pick. Our top pick. We had a go-to list if you weren't interested, but I wanted you. Ignore the chatter and keep a low profile. It'll blow over. It always does. In the meantime, Scarlet and I have to run across town for a King Corp. meeting. My assistant will show you to your office and introduce you to your office staff. I'm looking forward to a great season, Coach."

Coach...

Fuck, I love the sound of that.

My office may be next to Max's, but my heart is in the bowels of the arena. Always has been. Coaching became my dream when playing was taken away from me too early, but like most things in life, it happened, I adjusted, and eventually, I realized that this is the life I wanted.

Walking the corridors is familiar.

Some things are the same in every rink.

The smell of the ice. The chill in the air. The noises coming from below.

Home.

The thought brings my tired eyes some peace. Meanwhile, I search for a certain redheaded physical therapist with a sweet smile and wicked mouth while I familiarize myself with my new life. Because that's what coaching hockey is. *A life.* Not a job. Figuring out how to balance that with full-time fatherhood won't be easy, but I'm basically the luckiest motherfucker who ever walked these halls, so you won't catch me complaining.

A door opens down the hall, and two women laugh before a tiny wisp of a woman steps out into the hallway. She looks at me cautiously before passing by. I stop at the open door and watch silently as Brynlee cleans up after the woman who just left. The one I'm assuming is her roommate, Grace.

And damn. She's fucking stunning without any effort at all. Her soft, red hair is pulled back in a ponytail, showing only diamond studs that sparkle in each ear. Black pants mold to the curves of her legs, and a red Revolution tee barely hints at the strength and beauty she's hiding beneath it. She looks professional and yet, sexy as hell.

When she turns to find me watching, she sucks in a breath and lifts her hand to her heart. "Jesus, Deacon. You scared the shit out of me." Once she catches her breath, her eyes narrow and sharpen. "What are you doing down here?"

"I just signed my contract. I thought I'd give myself a tour." I step into the room and close the door behind me, then with a flick of my wrist, lock it for good measure.

Her emerald eyes sparkle as I prowl to her like a predator stalking his prey.

"Kinda ballsy coming down here, don't you think?" She takes two steps back until she bumps up against a therapy table and is forced to hold her ground.

Defiant eyes look up at me as I take her face in my hands, unable to resist the all-encompassing need to touch her. "What's your point, red?"

Brynlee's hands fist my shirt, and breathlessly, she lifts up on her toes.

"I forget," she utters before our lips crash together.

Each of us fighting for control.

Her hands run under my polo and up my sides, flattening against my chest.

"Fuck, Brynn . . ." I lick into her mouth. "Did you give

your notice?" I ask as I drag my tongue down her neck, desperate for more of this woman.

"Yes." She inhales when I scrape my teeth over her thrumming pulse, meeting my desperation with her own. "That's why I was in Max's office this morning. I'm done thirty days from yesterday. Why?"

Her nails score my skin, and I slide my hands to cup her ass in my palms before I boost her onto the table. "Because if you've already quit, this isn't sexual harassment, right?"

She yanks my head back by my hair and laughs in my face. "The only way this turns into sexual harassment is if you don't make me come right now, Coach."

I push my hand inside her pants and plunge two fingers into her tight fucking pussy and swallow her moan. "Like this?" I ask against her lips, adding a third finger and loving the way her body shakes.

"Yes . . ." she keens, trembling under my touch before I circle her clit, and get off on the way she cries out again. "Right there. Don't stop."

I take my orders and double down, wringing her orgasm from her body in minutes, then devour every sound that slips past her pouty lips until she's breathless beneath me. Her sex-drunk eyes widen as I pull my fingers from her pants and suck them clean. "Fucking perfect, red."

She blinks up at me slowly before she giggles the sexiest laugh I've ever heard.

"I swear to God, it's like there's a magnetic pull. Like I have no choice when it comes to you." She drags a lazy finger over my lips, wiping them clean.

"Good," I tell her, relieved to know this isn't a one-way thing, desperate to fuck her but positive that's not a good idea. Not here. Not now. "Come with me to Boston."

"What?" she stiffens. "Boston?"

"I've got a few things I have to take care of before I can

give the Revolution everything I've got. I'm going to be up there for a few weeks. Come with me. No one there knows you. They'll leave us alone..."

"Deacon," she chews on her bottom lip and shifts. "I wish I could, but I just gave my notice. I can't take the next few weeks off. My colleagues have summer vacations planned. I'm the only one here to cover for them. I can't do that. Not to Max. Not to the team."

I run my thumb along her jaw, disappointed. "You sure, Brynn?"

She turns her face and kisses my palm, sending a bolt of lust so damn hot and sharp through me that I swear this woman could bring me to my knees. "I wish I could. I really... *really* do. But I can't. Not now."

She looks up at me through long inky lashes. "When are you leaving?"

"When I'm done here." I cup her face in my hands and press my lips to her forehead. "Can I call you later?"

She lifts her face and ghosts her lips over mine. "I'll talk to you later, Coach."

The words don't feel like enough, but I don't have any other choice.

BRYNLEE

Sweating the stress out has always been my favorite form of therapy. Beating the hell out of a heavy bag was fun from the very first time my dad laced my first pair of pink boxing gloves on my hands and showed me proper form. Was it a little unconventional that this was my fourth birthday gift? *Yes*, yes it was. Did I think Mom was going to kill Dad when he did it? Also a resounding yes. But that didn't stop him from working with me for a few minutes every day until my form was perfect. Perfection never came. But I've been pretty damn close since sometime around age nine.

Child prodigy?

No. Definitely not.

More like a precocious kid who loved this gym more than any other building she's ever set foot in. Some things never change. And while the Revolution arena comes a very close second to Crucible, Crucible will always hold the title of my first love.

I think, deep down, I knew I'd end up right here one day, working with these fighters, but I wanted to hone my skill and earn my place like every other member of the team had to. I wanted to come here on my own terms, in my own time, and now it feels like my hand was forced.

Mom believes everything in our lives is the result of the effort we put in. But she's also the first one to try to pull the damn strings, even if we don't want her to. I guess I shouldn't have been surprised. But her actions hurt. And actions have consequences. She's always said that. Coming to terms with the consequences might not be easy for her, or me for that matter, but it is what it is now.

Dad likes to say everything happens for a reason, even if we're never privy to exactly what that reason is. Maybe there's a reason this is happening now. Maybe there isn't.

I've always fallen somewhere between their two lines of thinking.

I've put in the time and done the work. I'm an excellent physical therapist. I'm pissed my choice was taken from me. I can admit that to myself, if not to anyone else.

Maybe this is the kick I needed right now.

Maybe not.

Maybe it's all bullshit and I could have been happy with the Revolution for another ten years. Guess I'll never know. But while I'm heartbroken to leave my players, I'm trying to look at this as kismet. Maybe this thing with Deacon will turn into something or maybe it won't. Either way, knowing I won't be working under him in a month certainly makes the journey to figuring out what a relationship with him *could* look like *if* I chose one a whole lot easier.

And based on the magnetic pull that seems to be charged between us, I'm not sure there's any choice to be made.

These are the thoughts running through my head as I pound out my frustrations on the bag with true tunnel vision. So much so, I don't notice when my brother, Killian, walks up next to me until he pops one of my earbuds out of my ear, and I have to pull the jab I'm about to throw before I clip his jaw.

"Are you stupid?" I ask over the loud base of Linkin Park still playing in one ear. "I almost hit you."

"I know how to duck." He holds the little white AirPod in front of my face. "You're listening to old school. I like it. Who pissed you off?"

Killian is three years younger than me and an entire foot taller.

Does he have incredible reflexes? Of course he does. But mine are better.

I fake a jab, then stomp his foot, and he drops my AirPod into my glove.

Mission accomplished.

"It's probably easier to ask who hasn't pissed me off. Newsflash—your name wouldn't be on that list." I pull off one glove with my teeth, then unlace and yank off the other. "How's your new room, shithead?"

"Come on, Brynnie. It's not like I stole your room. You and Maddox made your agreement. That's not my fault. I just accepted an offer. You know I've been dying to get out of Mom and Dad's house." My brother might be six feet, four inches of lethally trained muscle, but he's still a big baby.

"Whatever you say, Killer. I hope you get crabs from sharing a bathroom with Callen." I wipe the sweat from my face with the back of my hand, then smack his chest. "Don't come crying to me when you need a shot of penicillin."

"Whatever." The ass pats my head with a condescendingly annoying grin. "Dad wants you in his office."

"You should have started with that," I tell him before walking away.

"Hey, you've got to clean the bag," he calls back.

"Looks like that's on you now. Dad wants me," I singsong back to him and walk down the hall to Dad's office.

This day started out so promising. But that was before I got proverbially bitchslapped, first by Isla, then by the Revolution. I'm not even sure how to classify the news that Deacon is going back to Boston. I know it's just a few weeks, but right now that feels like an eternity. I'm pretty sure this day can officially be classified as a shit show. At least that's what I'm calling it in my head when I walk up to Dad's closed door. Maybe that means I'm getting a reprieve.

A girl can hope.

I knock once and he yells, "Come in," right away.

Guess it's just not my day.

Time to face the music.

"Hi, Daddy."

Dad looks up from his computer, the same one I'm fairly sure he's had for twenty years because Cade St. James despises technology with a flaming, fiery, passion. He removes the black glasses he started to wear a few years ago and shakes his head before he bothers to stand up and open his arms for me to step into, like he's always done. Once he's wrapped me up in a sweaty hug, he rests his chin on the top of my head and breathes out a sigh.

"Love you, kid."

"Love you too, Dad," I tell him, knowing I need to hit him up for a job but not ready to break that ice just yet. Luckily, I don't have to wait long.

He pulls away and guides me to the seat across from his desk. Also the same one he's had for twenty years. "Now . . . You want to tell me what the hell changed between Friday night and now?"

I blink up at him quietly, knowing he's not done with me yet.

"When I went to bed Friday, I had a baby girl away at college, a son who lived at home, another baby girl living her best life in a penthouse condo, working as a physical therapist for the number one hockey team in the nation, and a happy wife." He scratches his graying temple, then glares. "Do you want to know what's changed?"

"Umm . . ." I don't dare tell him I know exactly what's changed. Not when he's already on a roll.

"Umm . . . sounds about right. Your brother moved out. Ironically, into your former penthouse. Your mother is pissed at the world, including me." He pauses for a minute and shakes his head again. "Why, you ask, is she pissed at me?"

"I didn't—"

"She's pissed at me because I apparently stole you from her after she moved you onto her staff from Max's staff. Pissed at me. I didn't even know I stole you. You gotta help me here, Brynnie, because I know I'm getting old, but I really didn't think I was so old that I forgot about you finally accepting the job offer to be our staff physical therapist." He sits his ass on the corner of his desk and grips the edge with rapidly whitening knuckles. "Did I miss anything else over the course of forty-eight hours, Brynlee?" His voice has gotten quiet as he's gone on, and that's never a good sign.

"Gracie moved back in with me for a few months," I tell him hesitantly, unsure if he's angry or just confused. It's kinda hard to tell.

"Okay, great. Add that to the list of rapidly changing events. Gracie Sinclair is back from London, and if I understand correctly, you're what . . . sharing your cousin Maddox's condo?"

I nod in agreement, not wanting to open my mouth again.

"Okay. So now that we're on the same page, can I ask a few questions and get a few straight answers from you? Because your mother isn't just mad at me. She's furious with you too. She says you won't talk to her. You ignored her yesterday and apparently walked right by her today when you gave Max your letter of resignation." Then his cheeks grow redder, and I'm a little concerned he's about to stroke out.

Oh, shit. I may have broken my dad.

"Oh. OH. Let's not forget your mother hired that little shit from Block Island to coach the Revolution and then told me he was making eyes at you this morning. This is the shit I'm getting called about, Bryn. I'm gonna need your help here, kid."

Every muscle in my body locks because of all the things I was expecting him to throw my way, that last one wasn't it.

When I don't respond, he moves into the seat next to me. "So how about we start with you working here?"

His words may seem calmer now than a moment ago, but it's not often that Dad loses his shit, and I'm still treading carefully, waiting for another bomb to blow.

"You didn't forget anything. I was just hoping your offer to work here still stands because I'd like to join the Crucible family." Okay. That wasn't so hard.

"Kid." He takes my hand in his. "You *are* the Crucible family. If you're ready to work here, I couldn't be happier. But I want you to think about it. Because working here just to piss off your mother isn't a good enough reason."

"That's not it. I promise. Mom switched me over to the Kings without talking to me about it. She did it without my consent. And while I understand I'm her little girl and she thinks she knows best, she doesn't get to make that choice for me anymore. I'm a grown woman, Dad. I haven't lived at home in years. I don't ask you guys for anything. I earn my own money. Pay my own bills. Earned my own degrees. And live my own life," I argue. "I loved my job. And I'm damn good at it. I decided the timing was finally right for me to work at Crucible, and I gave them my notice. That's the story." Maybe not every single detail but all the details he needs to know.

"What if Max told you that you could stay on with the Revolution with no chance of you ever being moved to the Kings? Would you still want to work here? Because Max is willing to add that to your contract to get you to stay." Yup. Knew there was another bomb waiting to be tossed.

I think about that.

Would I stay?

I look around this office and smile at the pictures covering Dad's walls. So much of our history in one room. I guess my answer is pretty easy. "No. It's time. I'm ready to work for Crucible."

"Well that's one thing done then. You're hired. But before you go jumping up to hug me, I want more answers, and your mother isn't giving them to me. So it's your turn. How the hell did you end up trading condos?"

I sit, filling Dad in on the rest of the weekend.

Well, not all of it, but all I'm willing to share.

It's not until he's hugging me goodbye that he squeezes my shoulder and looks away. "Have you thought any more about getting tested, Brynn?"

I shake my head and kiss his cheek. "Love you, Dad. See you soon."

It's not the answer he wants, but it's the only one he's getting today.

DEACON

"Slow down, brother. So now she's going to give you full custody of Kennedy?" Ripley kicks his legs up on my balcony and pops the top open on his beer. I wasn't expecting him when he knocked on my door earlier tonight, but I probably should have been surprised he managed to wait a few days before he showed up here. "I mean, I'm kinda surprised Isla wasn't more of a bitch about it."

I lean against the railing and look over at the harbor. Definitely gonna miss this view. "She's not a bitch, Rip. She's trying to do what's right for Kennedy. We all are. It's just not easy." Anxiety is a bitch, and my poor kid has been dealing with it her whole life.

The fucker chokes on his beer. "If she was doing what's best for Kennedy, she wouldn't be going to Japan."

"You know it's not that simple," I argue, but he mimes like he's jerking off.

He was never a big Isla fan.

"Remind me why the hell you came back from Jersey?" I ask as I flick my beer cap at him.

"Beer's better in Boston. And I couldn't let you say goodbye to this place alone. We had some good times here."

"You mean before you got traded to Nashville," I goad him, knowing he fucking hates his new team.

"Listen, asshole. I'm a free agent as of a month ago. I can go anywhere I want if the offer's right, and coming back to Boston is top on my list of wants." He looks at me over his beer. "Now tell me what's top on *your* list of wants."

I turn around and lean against the wrought iron, leaving the city and the bay at my back. "What do I want? Well, Doctor Phil, let's talk about what I want."

Fuck . . . it's been so fucking long since I've let myself really think about what I want, I'm not even sure where to start.

"I want Kennedy to be happy. I want to make sure she's taken care of and happy. I want my daughter to not be in a constant state of stress and anxiety that has her closing in on herself, shrinking her world until it's just her in a room, alone." My jaw clenches at the thought of that happening again. Because it wasn't all that long ago that my little girl had a breakdown when she had to switch schools, and I never want to see that happen to her again.

"I want Isla to trust me with Kennedy. Fuck . . . I want to trust *myself* with her. I want to trust that I'm making the right decisions for her. And how the hell am I supposed to do that when I'm going to be away from her for half a season?" I crack my neck, my frustration growing higher and higher until it's at a boiling point. "I don't know how I'm gonna do it, man. How am I gonna leave her?"

"Okay, breathe, brother. Don't go stroking out on me. We'll find you one of those nannies everybody has. Maybe we can get a hot one, and she can take care of Kennedy *and* you." He laughs like a fucking perv. "Seriously though, you're going to need help with my goddaughter, and it's going to have to be someone she's comfortable with and someone who's going to stick around, so you're minimizing the change she's dealing with as much as possible. Bonus points if she's hot."

"I'm not screwing any nanny, dipshit," I argue, and a vision of Brynlee plays in my mind from my last night in Kroydon Hills.

"Well, *now* you're thinking of something that doesn't involve your kid. Because that face isn't PG, dude."

I finally laugh because seriously, only a good friend can go there.

"Did you meet a girl?" he teases, like a teenager.

"What the fuck are you? A high school girl?"

"Is she why you blew me off at the bar last week?" Rip digs in like a dog with a bone. "I sense a story here. Seriously, Deacon, man, it's like I'm psychotic."

I drop down into the seat across from him and shove his feet off my goddamn table. "It's psychic, shithead."

"That's not a no though."

Ripley is one of those guys I met in the minors when I was a teenager. We were both placed with the same family in Canada one year, and I haven't been able to get rid of him since. At least that's what I like to tell him. In reality, he's the closest thing to a brother I've ever had. And shithead or not, he's been there for me through it all. My marriage, my divorce, the birth of my daughter. He was there when my dreams of playing pro blew up in my face, and the fucker flew halfway across the damn country to watch my first game as the head coach at Boston University. He acts like an idiot, but it's an act . . . I think.

"I wouldn't say I met her as much as we bumped into each other for the first time in years." And fuck, just thinking of her makes me wish I was in Kroydon Hills instead of Boston.

"I knew her when we were kids. She was younger than me, though, and her dad told me to stay away."

"And you listened? What the fuck, man? Since when can an old man scare you away from something you want?"

I finish my beer, then set it on the table and pull two more out of the box at our feet. I wait to hand him his until he empties his bottle, then lean back. "Since her old man is Cade St. James."

"No shit . . . The Saint? I saw him fight once in a charity thing when I was in high school. It was him and Hudson Kingston. They raised a ton of money for some foundation. Dude was probably forty years old, and that motherfucker was still jacked. Damn . . . I'd have stayed away too." He leans forward and grins a cocky fucking grin. "What changed now? You think you can take him?"

My body shakes with a silent laugh. "No. It was just . . . I don't know, man. There's something about this girl. She's . . . I can't put it into words. There's something there. Something I can't stop thinking about."

"I bet she's pretty, right?" He lifts his eyebrows and waits for an answer.

"She's incredible," I tell him, unwilling to share anything else. Not when it comes to Brynlee.

"Better add her to the list then," Rip tells me. His chest puffs up, proud of himself for thinking of it.

And he's right. Brynlee St. James is at the top of the list of things I want for myself.

> **DEACON**
> How's the countdown to unemployment going?

> **BRYNLEE**
> Ha ha ha. Very funny. I have a new job lined up.

> **DEACON**
> Did you talk to your dad?

> **BRYNLEE**
> I did. I'll start for him once I'm done with the Revolution.

> **DEACON**
> And you're sure you want to leave?

> **BRYNLEE**
> I wish it had happened differently, but, I'm sure. How are your loose ends? All tied up?

> **DEACON**
> Not yet. I got my place listed with a realtor and already had a few people come through. Ripley stopped by the other night to say goodbye to the old place. But I have a few more things to take care of with the university before I'm done there.

> **BRYNLEE**
> How are things with Isla and Kennedy?

> **DEACON**
> Not a conversation I feel like having over text.

I hit the FaceTime option and wait for Brynn to answer, but when she does, I wish I'd done it sooner. Her strawberry hair is piled high in a bun on top of her head, and bubbles cover her body. Her phone must be resting on something because she's got a glass of wine in one hand, and she's not holding the phone with the other.

"You didn't tell me you were naked, red." My voice is thick with want already. It only takes a split-second with this woman.

Her lips curve up behind her glass of red wine. "Sorry, Coach. I was unaware I had to tell you I was soaking in a tub while I was texting with you."

"I mean, you don't have to, but it definitely makes the texting more interesting," I tell her before I lean back against my headboard. "What were you doing before I called?"

"Reading . . ." she answers coyly.

The blush that just rose up those pale cheeks tells a different story. "Reading what?"

"Grace and Everly's aunt writes steamy romances. I just downloaded her newest book."

"Steamy, huh?" I tease, wanting to know more. "Tell me about it."

"Deacon—"

"Brynlee, I'm trying to get to know you. I told you what I read before bed. Now it's your turn."

She sips her wine and hides behind her glass. "It's about a football player falling in love with an heiress."

"You into football players, St. James?" Even saying that turns my fucking stomach. Apparently, when it comes to Brynlee, I'm a greedy son of a bitch, because I don't even want some Fabio wanna-be to be her type.

"Not since a certain hockey coach caught my attention. Does it make me sound needy if I say I miss you? I mean, what the hell? I didn't see you for a decade. How can I miss you? That sounds ridiculous, doesn't it?" she stammers in that adorable way she does when she gets nervous, and yeah, it probably shouldn't, but it makes my dick hard.

"Hey, now. You're talking to the guy who asked you to come to Boston with him. None of this really makes sense. But it doesn't need to if it feels right to us." I've done the relationship that made perfect sense before and ended up divorced. Just because something sounds good on paper doesn't mean it's good.

She puts her glass down out of my line of sight and leans back against some pillowy-looking thing as a strand of long hair spills down by her face. "I like that you're in this with me, Deacon. I like that you're man enough—*confident* enough—that you don't make me feel stupid for saying something like that."

"I'll be back soon, Brynn, and when I get back, I'll show you just how much I can make it feel right." I lick my bottom lip, fucking hungry for her. "Where's your hand, Brynlee?"

Her sexy little smile tips up on one side. "Wherever you want it to be, Deacon."

"I want you to play with your clit, red. Circle it with your fingers, but don't touch. Not yet."

She moans softly as her hand moves under the bubbles. "I'd rather it was your hand."

Fuck me.

I want all her orgasms.

"Soon, baby. Until then, you're going to have to listen to me." I fist my own cock under my shorts and enjoy the way my little redhead blushes so fucking easily. "I want you to trace that pretty pussy, baby. Just drag one finger up and down."

"More, Deacon . . ." she whispers with her eyes locked on mine. Her other hand comes up out of the water and squeezes her breast that's playing peak-a-boo with the bubbles. Her pale pink nipple peeks through, making my mouth water at the idea that there's so much I'm not seeing. But my God, what I *am* seeing is fucking beautiful.

"Show me how you fuck yourself, baby. Show me what you'd want me to do if I was there," I order her. And damn... what a sight. She arches her back while the bubbles slosh around her, the flicker of candlelight illuminating her gorgeous, flushed face.

"I need you, Deacon," she whimpers.

"Soon, red. I'll be back soon. And when I get back, I'm going to worship your perfect body all night long. I'm going to fuck you for hours without letting you come. And when I finally do, you're going to soak my fucking sheets. You're going to feel me between your legs for fucking days, beautiful. Now come, Brynlee."

The prettiest goddamn moan leaves her pursed lips as her eyes flutter closed, and fuck my life . . . Who gives a shit that I just came in my boxers like a damn teenager? I could die a happy man—right now, right here. With the picture of Brynlee St. James's face the last damn thing I ever see.

Brynlee

LINDY

Are we allowed to acknowledge the fact that Everly is pregnant yet?

GRACIE

I mean she told me.

BRYNLEE

She didn't tell me, but I guessed a few weeks ago.

EVERLY

How did you guess?

BRYNLEE

You're kidding, right?

LINDY

Hello, coffee snob . . . you're drinking decaf. Dead giveaway.

KENZIE

Are you kidding me!!! One of us is a licensed ob-gyn, and I have to find out you're pregnant from a group text message? You guys seriously suck.

LINDY

We love you, Kenz. I'm sure we'll still be having babies when you're done with your residency.

EVERLY

You go right ahead, Lindy. I think Cross and I may stop at three. We'll be outnumbered.

LINDY

You say that now, but you like his dick way too much to stop so soon.

KENZIE

Birth control, Lindy. Let me know if you need some.

EVERLY

His dick is really pretty. It has the perfect curve.

LINDY

I love Easton's dick. It's definitely my favorite toy. Big and thick . . .

KENZIE

Please, God. Stop. A sister just doesn't need to know.

LINDY

I'm just doing it to drive you nutty, Kenz. You know you'd miss it if I didn't.

EVERLY

I'm calling it now. I'm stopping at three.

GRACIE

Mom and Dad always said they had enough for a football team.

EVERLY

Yup and all the boys play hockey.

BRYNLEE

It is a far superior sport.

LINDY

Don't let Callen hear you say that.

GRACIE

She'd have to be talking to Callen or Maddox for him to hear that.

EVERLY

You're still not talking to them?

BRYNLEE

Nope. Maddox is a big fat jerk.

KENZIE

Oh no. The language. I mean . . . jerk? That's pretty bad, Brynnie.

BRYNLEE

Shut up. I'm not over it yet.

LINDY

Do you mean the boys haven't even come over to raid the fridge? They did that daily.

> **GRACIE**
> I mean, Nixon is in and out every day, and Killian sneaks in and raids the fridge. But he makes sure Brynlee isn't home.
>
> **BRYNLEE**
> You traitor. You let my brother eat our food! He stole my room.
>
> **GRACIE**
> He's like a cute little stray dog, Brynn. Don't make me kick the dog.
>
> **LINDY**
> OMG. Did you guys hear that Lenny's dog's puppies are old enough to find homes?
>
> **EVERLY**
> Wait . . . Lenny is still breeding bulldogs?
>
> **LINDY**
> Yes! I swear instead of a cat lady, she's going to be a dog lady. And you know Bash can't tell her no.
>
> **EVERLY**
> I may have to work on Cross to get a puppy.
>
> **KENZIE**
> Cross gave you a baby. Focus on one thing at a time.

I close out of our text messages and call my aunt. I think it's time for a puppy.

BRYNLEE

I should have known my mother wouldn't wait for me to come to her. It's been nearly two weeks, and I've ignored more summonses than I can count. And maybe that's not fair. It makes her sound like an evil queen ruling over her court with an iron fist.

That's not her.

First of all, she'd never be caught dead with iron.

It's platinum all the way for Scarlet Kingston-St. James.

That thought makes me smile enough to walk into my office with Winnie by my side. I ignore the fact that she's sitting behind my desk with her legs crossed and her red-soled heel tapping against the tile floor.

"Good morning, Brynlee." She's doing a fabulous job of hiding the annoyance I know she's feeling.

"Morning, Mom," I answer as I walk around my desk and hang up my bag, then unbuckle Winnie's collar and add a new chew toy to her bed in the corner of my office.

"What is that?" she asks, staring at Winnie.

I look down at my brand-new baby and smile. "Mother, meet Winston Churchill. Winnie, meet Grandma."

"Bite your damn tongue, Brynlee. I'm not a grandma. We need to come up with a much better name." She reaches her hand down and runs her palm over Winnie's soft fur, then shakes her head. "Winston Churchill?"

I bend over and pour a bottle of water in her bowl and laugh at the way she's curled up next to Mom's silk pantsuit, and my God, she's definitely leaving hair everywhere. "Yes, Winston Churchill. I'm calling her Winnie for short. She kinda looks like him, don't you think?"

Mom laughs until Winnie starts chewing her purse. "Your aunt and the dogs. I swear. You'd think she was an animal lover when in reality, it's only bulldogs."

"I know you didn't come here to talk to me about Winnie, Mom. And I need to boot up my computer so I can start my day."

"Well, I need to talk to my daughter. So it seems if you do what *I* want, then I'll be able to get up so you can do what *you* want. Win-win." Her perfectly painted red lips stretch into a triumphant smile, and I have about half a second to decide whether I feel like dealing with the fallout of leaving the Revolution to work for Crucible.

But as it turns out, luck is on my side.

Nixon Sinclair knocks on my open door, then looks between Mom, Winnie, and me. "Hey, Brynn. Do you have time for me?"

Saved by the Sinclair.

"Come on in, Nix. I've got you on my schedule." I look over at my mother without saying a word.

"Hey, Mrs. St. James," Nixon says like a twelve-year-old boy who probably thought my mom was hot instead of a grown man who was just drafted to the best damn team in the National Hockey League. Then he moves into the room and grabs a treat from the glass jar that sits on my desk and squats down in front of my dog to get her love.

"Good morning, Nixon." Mom rises from the desk and picks up her Birkin bag. "You can't keep shutting me out, Brynlee," she warns warmly. Probably more warmly than I deserve, but she's in the wrong here, and that's a hill I'm willing to die on.

I shut the door behind my mom and turn to Nix, who's currently on the floor with Winnie in his lap. "Come on, Nix. Hop up on the table and let me grab the massage gun."

Winnie licks his face before he moves her back to her bed and takes off his shirt. "You doing okay, Brynn? I was surprised to hear you were leaving the Revolution."

I grab the gun and run it over Nixon's lower back as the knot in my stomach grows. It always does when I think about leaving. "It was time. But you know this team is my first love and always will be."

Nix groans as the gun goes over a particularly sensitive area.

"One day, some lucky fucker is going to bump the team down to second place, Brynn. But he's going to have to go through all of us first."

"If you weren't my best friends' little brother, I'd think you were hitting on me, Nixon Sinclair," I tease, knowing that's not what he's doing but wanting to break the serious turn this conversation just took. Especially because the man who immediately comes to mind is Nixon's new coach.

"Nah. Just looking out for one of our own."

"Well that goes both ways. I hope the woman lucky enough to catch your eye is worthy of such a great guy. You're one in a million, Nix."

I shake my head and loosen him up before we start the rest of his session.

Hopefully, the guys won't be too pissed when and if they find out about Deacon.

Jesus. How many secrets can I continue to keep?

BRYNLEE

If distance makes the heart grow fonder, time makes the heart grow horny.

—Brynlee's Secret Thoughts

I've learned more about Deacon Kane than I may even know about myself. That's what texting, talking, and FaceTime phone sex every night like two teenagers living six hours apart will do for you.

His favorite food is pizza.

His favorite word is *fuck*. Something we happen to have in common. I did grow up in an MMA gym, after all. For Deacon, it's a noun, pronoun, verb, adjective, and a proper noun. It also sounds sexy as hell coming out of his mouth when he's groaning it when he sees what I'm wearing to bed on FaceTime. I may have gone a little overboard with my lingerie shopping since I realized this. But what can I say . . . it's fun to see his reaction.

According to him, he and Isla are very good friends now. But it took a while for that to happen. Learning to co-parent was always easy, but it seems to be going well. At least for the time being. That is until tonight.

"I don't understand." I wrap my cardigan around myself and rest my hand holding the phone on my knees. "I thought she already planned to go to Japan with Shaun."

"She's really worried about how my schedule is going to affect Kennedy. And we haven't agreed on any of the prospective nannies I sent her." He runs his hand through his dark hair, and I silently wish I'd gone to Boston with him, just so I could be there for him. "She's had an issue with each resume. I don't know what the hell I'm going to do."

"What did your parents say?" I ask, knowing he was stopping to see them today before driving back to Kroydon Hills tomorrow.

"My mom said she could help a little. But let's be realistic. They have a business that takes both of them to run. Their life is on Block Island, and I just signed a contract with the Revolution. My life will be in Philadelphia. Unless I ask to be let out of my contract, I have to find someone to help me in Kroydon Hills."

"Deacon." I cringe at that thought. "You can't do that. This is a great opportunity for you. Max could have hired anyone to come in and take over this team, and he chose you. Don't give up on that yet. You've got time. Even if you don't have a nanny in place before Isla leaves, you still have over a month before preseason games start. Hell, your practices don't even start until next month. You've got time to figure this out."

He sighs and drops his head into his hands. "Yeah. I just don't know. I told Isla we'd talk tomorrow when I get back to town. Are you working tomorrow?"

"I am." Even though I wish I wasn't, but I don't tell him that. "I've got one more week to go before I start at Crucible."

"I promised Kennedy I'd take her shopping once I'm home tomorrow, but I need to fucking see you, red. I need to touch you and not be stuck behind a goddamned screen."

A nervous zing of anticipation runs down my body. "Is that your way of asking me on a date, Deacon?"

"It's my way of saying let me cook you dinner the night after, then let me eat you for dessert. Come to my house. Pack a bag. And let's not get out of bed for a few fucking days."

Holy hotness . . . this man.

Yes, please.

"I'm working with Gracie in the morning and have a few appointments later in the afternoon. I'm not sure exactly what the next few days look like." Except maybe I'll be squeezing in one more trip to Le Désir lingerie shop.

"Good, baby. Because I promised Kennedy I'd take her shopping, but then I want you in my bed all weekend."

Who am I to say no to that?

A few hours later, I get settled on my couch with Sweet Temptations s'mores cupcake. A girl has to have her vices, and chocolate and caffeine are mine. I'm also that girl who likes her air-conditioning cranked low so she can be under a blanket. Which is why I'm tucked under a blanket in the corner of our couch with my iPad out when Maddox waltzes into the condo like he owns the place.

I spin to my knees and lean over the back of the couch as he makes his way into the kitchen. "Hey, asshole. You moved. You don't get a key."

"Not how this works, Brynnie. I raided your fridge when

you lived upstairs, and you let me. No changing the rules now." He looks in my Sweet Temptations bag and hums when he sees Aunt Amelia's cupcakes.

"Ohh. These are my favorite."

"Maddox, I'm going to kill you," I growl like a feral fucking cat.

"You won't be the first or last to try." He pulls out a cookie and a mint chocolate-chip cookie cupcake. "You don't even like mint chip. You know you bought this for me."

I turn back around and tuck myself back under the soft white blanket.

Of course he's right. I always get the damn mint chip because whenever I stop, I get enough for all of us, the guys included. Especially since it was just me in the condo after Kenzie moved out until Gracie came back.

The shit sits down next to me with his cupcake, his cookie, and a glass of milk, then picks up the remote. "Did you see that new Brat Pack documentary yet? It just came out last week. Looks pretty good."

I steal the remote and the cookie right out of his hand and break off half, then take a sip of his milk too, just because I know he won't stop me, and I want to be a pain in his ass. Once I'm satisfied, I hand him the remote but hold it out of reach. "Why didn't you just tell me about my mom, Maddox?"

He dunks the cookie in his milk, because he knows I'll never eat it after that, and stretches his legs up on the ottoman. "I would have told you either way, Brynn. But I've been trying to get you to swap condos for months." He pops the whole fucking cookie in his mouth, then washes it down with the rest of the milk before he turns to me. "You didn't need all that space. I did."

"You didn't need it. You and Callen were fine in here," I argue, refusing to let him off that easy.

"Listen . . . Killian has been wanting to move out for months—"

"Stop . . . Just stop." I give in and drop the remote on his lap.

"Brynnie—You can't be mad at me," he pouts, and I actually laugh. His father is the head of the Philadelphia Mafia, and he just pouted because I'm pissed.

"Fine," I give in. "I guess you're right. I can't be mad. Especially after the conversation I had with your mom when I picked up my coffee and cupcakes today." I lift my brows and bite down on my lip, knowing this is going to be good.

He turns on the TV and brings up the apps list, searching for the documentary. "What conversation?"

Now it's my turn to enjoy the torture.

The beauty of growing up so close to your cousins might be always having them by your side, but that also means you know how to hit them where it hurts the hardest when they're least expecting it. When we were little, Maddox hated having the hair on his arm pulled.

Today, I may as well have pulled them all out, one by one.

Madman stiffens beside me. "What. Conversation. Brynn?"

"Oh, just the one I had with Aunt Amelia, telling her about our condo swap. I made sure she knew it was your idea and that you really pushed for it because you're such an amazing brother that you wanted to be able to look out for Caitlin."

Maddox opens his mouth, about to cut me off, but I don't let him.

"You see, your mom and dad really don't like that Caitlin is stuffed into a three-bedroom apartment with Ares and Nixon and that Bellamy and she are sharing a room. But oh man, did your mom love hearing that you were going to let Caitlin and Bellamy take the two extra rooms in the penthouse." I pat his back and smile slowly and sweetly before I take the remote from him and hit play on the show. "Your mom is super proud of you, by the way."

Maddox grinds his teeth before he picks his cupcake back up and pops the whole damn thing in his mouth. He takes his time chewing, then finally looks at me with a shake of his head. "Well played, Brynnie. Well played."

"Checkmate, Madman. Checkmate."

BRYNLEE

Murder podcasts are as close to an actual crime as I'll ever get. I'm too much of a coffee whore to survive in prison, and the way my hair sheds, there'd be traces of my DNA everywhere.

—Brynlee's Secret Thoughts

DEACON

You awake, red?

Am I awake?

The better question would be why does that one single word, even if it's just in a text, send goosebumps dancing down my arms? Oh right. Because it's Deacon saying it.

BRYNLEE

Barely. It's been a long day. How did shopping go?

DEACON

Kennedy seemed to enjoy some of it, so that's a win. She's going to bring a lot of her things from Isla's house. My kid's probably one of the few little girls in the world whose skin crawls at the thought of a room full of new things. She doesn't really like shopping. Everything Isla picked up Kennedy hated.

I think it's the idea of moving here that she hates.

BRYNLEE

I'm sure it's the idea of the move, not the idea of living with you that's bothering her.

I turn on my side and then swipe the FaceTime option, *needing* to see him.

He's been gone for days, and it's felt like so much longer.

Stupid fucking emotions.

How can I be so desperate to see a man I hadn't seen in years until last month?

"Hey," he answers softly with a beautiful rasp to his voice. "I'm sorry I didn't get to see you tonight. Kennedy asked me to read with her before bed, and we went for a few chapters since we're getting close to the end." He runs his fingers along his jaw, and I stare at the veins bulging there, unsure I've ever found hands sexier than I do right now. "What are you thinking about, crazy girl?"

"Nothing," I murmur, attempting to ignore how incredibly hot I find this man.

"How about you come over here and tell me that." And damn, that voice is not helping things at all.

"I'm already in bed," I tease and flash the camera over my body, lying in my cool sheets, wearing nothing but a cropped tank and cheeky panties.

"Wait," he stops me, and the heat in his eyes is molten. "Slow down with the camera. Let me enjoy the view."

The sound that catches is sleepy and more than a little turned-on. "Shame you're not here to see it in person, husband," I tease, enjoying the way he reacts to the sight of me. I'm not sure I've ever felt possessive over a man before, but I could definitely see myself being possessive over this one.

"Give me your address, Brynlee," he orders, and why . . . Why does that sound sexy?

"You can't come here, Deacon. My roommate is home, and I'm pretty sure she's banging one of your players in her room." Grace and I are definitely rocking the whole *don't ask, don't tell* philosophy at the moment.

The difference is Grace is avoiding confirming or denying she's dating her sister's new brother-in-law, whereas I'm banging his new coach.

I'm so screwed.

"I have ways of finding you, baby" he warns.

My body heats.

"Are you listening to me? Ares Wilder is sleeping in the room next to mine. You can't come here." I shake my head as my frustration builds, and the walls that were so easily fortified only a few days ago already start to crumble because I want him to be here. Screw the consequences.

"My place or yours, red. Choice is yours."

"Doesn't sound like I have much of a choice." I lie flat on my back and move the phone, giving Deacon an incredible angle of my boobs. Maybe I'm a little evil, but the growl that leaves him is my new favorite sound.

"Oh, you have a choice. Make me hunt down your address and it will be days before I let you come again."

My breath catches in my throat.

"And the other option?" I whisper as I bend my knees and press my thighs together to relieve some of the pressure.

"Oh, baby. Give me your address, and I'll show you."

This man is going to destroy all my walls.

I just hope, in the end, I'm not the one destroying him.

The quiet condo is bathed in darkness when Deacon texts, letting me know he's outside my door. I tiptoe past Gracie's quiet room and offer up a silent prayer that my friend and her man don't decide to get a midnight snack right now. This is such a bad idea, but like a sweet addiction I can't control, I need my next hit more than my next breath, and Deacon Kane is my drug of choice.

I fluff my hair and fix my boobs, so they sit high in my cropped tank, then open the door. Any hesitation I may have had is washed away in an instant as a sudden, overwhelming need engulfs me. Deacon's dark blue eyes run over my body, like a heavy hand skimming every curve. "Jesus, red. You're a fucking masterpiece."

He steps inside the foyer, and we reach at the same time.

His knees bend, and his hands clasp my face as the kiss happens, hard and fast.

Two people desperate for one another.

His tongue invades my mouth, and my hands shove under his shirt, frantic to feel the warmth of his skin. Deacon slides one hand under my ass and lifts me off my feet as he carries me to the couch.

"Deacon . . ." I pull my mouth from his. "What are you doing. My room is the first one down the hall. The door is open," I whisper. "But please be quiet. This isn't how I want you to meet Grace and Ares."

"This room is farther away from your roommate, isn't it?" He sits down with me in his lap and drags his lips around the shell of my ear. "I thought your Grace was doing my player on the down-low. How do you know it's him?"

There's no holding back my laugh. "Doing your player?"

He runs his hands up my ribs, under my tank then palms my breasts with his deliciously callused palms. "I don't give a fuck about where any of my players are sleeping right now, red. I haven't seen you in days, and you answer your door dressed like every fucking teenage fantasy I ever had come to fucking life . . . You can't honestly expect me to give a flying fuck about anyone but you right now."

I pull off his backward Boston U hat and toss it to the side table, so I can run my fingers through his dark hair. "I missed you too, Coach."

I reach into Deacon's sweatpants and fist his cock, then push his pants down, frantic for his weight against me. Dying for him.

We're a ticking timebomb, just waiting for the fuse to burn down so it detonates around us both.

Deacon drags my tank over my head and spreads his palm between my shoulder blades as he settles between my legs and drags his cock along my sex, wrenching a needy cry from my throat.

"Don't play with me, Deacon . . . I need you."

His lips capture mine tenderly as he pushes up agonizingly slow while I slide down his cock, taking him inside me. "You've got me," he swears against my lips as he pulls out, just enough to leave me desperate for more, before slamming me back down on him. "You've got all of me in a way I never thought would be possible." His hands are everywhere as his mouth covers mine. "Completely, red."

Our bodies slide against each other, my nipples graze his hard chest with each lift of my hips. His fist pulls my hair, giving him the perfect angle to worship my body with his mouth. Licking up my neck as his thumb drags over my nipple. And, *oh God*, I throw my head back on a silent moan before turning my mouth back to his.

My orgasm crashes over me with an intensity that steals my breath and scorches my soul, just as Deacon whispers my name over and over into the darkness.

I lie naked, draped over Deacon's bare chest, enjoying the feel of his body under mine in that sweet spot between sleep and consciousness, when I feel his lips graze my jaw. "You still coming over tonight, baby?"

My smile is instant. "If you still want me to."

He lifts my face to his and brushes his lips over mine. "I always fucking want you, Brynn."

The blanket cocooning us falls away, and I wrap my arms around his shoulders.

"Oh shit."

I look up and see Ares Wilder standing in the living room and hide my body against Deacon's chest. "Sorry. Just leaving," Ares apologizes as he covers his face.

"Get out," I yell, and he walks blindly toward the door with his hand in front of his face.

"Oh my God," I half cry, half laugh. "Well, that was Ares."

"Guess he's another player I'm going to make puke." Deacon fucking laughs. "Swear to God, Brynn. I'm done hiding this."

"We're not hiding, so much as just not broadcasting it

yet," I try to reassure him. I drop my forehead to his. Let's get through this weekend then we'll deal with the rest."

Deacon drags the blanket back up my body. "Can we try to make sure none of my other players see you naked? I'd hate to want to kill them all."

DEACON

"Does it have a pool?" Kennedy asks through my phone as I stand in the cereal aisle of the grocery store, waiting for her to tell me what she wants. "Mom and Shaun always say no when I ask if we can get a pool."

I pinch the bridge of my nose as I stare at all the chocolate cereal options in front of me. "Listen, kid. It's on the lake. It doesn't have a pool. But it does have a kitchen with bowls and spoons. So I'm going to need you to tell me what kind of cereal you want me to buy."

I haven't even made it back to the house yet.

Not sure why I thought it would be a good idea to grocery shop before I get there.

Now I'm just hungry and frustrated in a store full of people.

This is why God invented online shopping.

Fuck this shit.

"I don't eat cereal anymore. Mom said it's not good for me. She's on a protein shake kick again, and between you and me, they're really gross." I can picture the look on her face so clearly, she could be standing next to me. Kennedy is really particular about what she'll eat and has always been on the small side. We're constantly talking to the pediatrician about her not gaining weight. That's why when we find something she'll actually eat, I let her have it. Even if it's chocolate cereal.

"Okay. Got it. Mom's protein shakes suck. I'll see what I can do about it." I add three different chocolate cereals to my cart, knowing she's eaten each of them before. Can't hurt to have them in the pantry. "Got any snack requests?" I ask as I move on to the next aisle.

She answers, "Popcorn," just as my hand reaches for the box of microwave popcorn I always keep at my house for her and grab two just to be on the safe side. "Can I have apples too?"

"Already grabbed a few." I add a bag of Doritos for myself and turn down the next aisle.

"Did you get the Granny Smiths?" she asks, like this is my first rodeo.

"I did. And I'll make sure it's the good peanut butter too," I assure her.

"Creamy, not chunky," she adds.

"Yup." I might not have gotten to spend every day of Kennedy's life in the same house as her, but my kid will never wonder whether her father is paying attention to her. She has always been my first priority, and I want her to feel that with every action, even if it's something as small as knowing her favorite peanut butter.

"Thanks, Dad." She's quiet while I pick out steaks for tonight, waiting on the other end of the phone for me to finish speaking to the butcher. "So . . . Mom said I'm going to meet your girlfriend this weekend."

Damn it, Isla.

I haven't even discussed our plans with Brynlee, and now

I'm talking about them with Kennedy at the grocery store. I wasn't even sure if we were really going for this weekend, but I guess that answers that.

"Are you okay with that?" I ask before confirming anything, unsure of the protocol here since I've never introduced anyone to Kennedy before.

"Does it matter if I'm not?"

My kid is nine going on nineteen.

"Yes. It will always matter," I reassure her, looking around to make sure I'm not drawing attention to myself. "Your feelings will always matter to me."

"I guess it's fine. But I don't know her, so it's kinda weird."

"The best way to get to know someone is to spend time with them, sweetheart. But your mom and Shaun and I will all be there with you." So not the fucking conversation I want to be having in public.

Kennedy is quiet for a little too long for my liking. "Do you not want to meet her?"

"No," she's quick to answer. "It's just . . . *different.*"

"Different isn't always bad."

"I know. But . . . I'm not gonna call her mom."

"Ken—" My words get stuck in my throat. This kid is getting so much thrown at her right now. "You have a mother. And she's incredible. But the same way that you have me as your awesome dad and love Shaun as your stepdad, you can have Mom as your mom, and you can like Brynlee without feeling guilty for it." Holy fucking hell, I'm dodging bullets left and right, and it's barely noon.

"I guess," she muses, less than enthused. "Can we get a dog?"

And just like that, the subject changes, and I add a few bottles of wine and some beer to my cart. I think I'm going to need a drink by the end of today.

I wouldn't call myself a relocation pro, but I've done it enough in my life to be comfortable in a new home pretty quickly. And this house makes it easier than any before it. The Kingstons have set me up in the exact lakefront home Brynlee said they would. A one-year lease, covered by King Corp., is in my contract with the option to buy at any point during that time. I'm grateful Hunter thought to have that part added because this place is great. It's got character, space, a view, and one hell of a security system.

It's a mix between high-end and homey. Reclaimed wood beams stretch across vaulted ceilings, and whites, grays, blues, and greens dominate most spaces but don't feel untouchable. An interior designer's hand is on every inch. And they clearly have better taste than I ever could, so I'm happy to appreciate it and happier that there's very little I have to change in this five-bedroom, six-bathroom beast of a house. With a home gym, theater room, and an office with floor-to-ceiling bookshelves and one of those ladders on wheels attached, no luxury has been missed.

It's also got a balcony that wraps around the entire second and third floors of the house which I plan on bending Brynlee over when she gets here tonight.

But first things first. I finish unloading the groceries, making mental notes of the things I missed. Like paper plates and napkins. Staples in my life because seriously, does anyone actually enjoy doing dishes?

I've just finished seasoning the steaks when a knock on the glass kitchen door catches my attention, especially when

I look up and find a familiar face standing on the other side, holding a six pack of beer in one hand and a tray of cookies in the other.

I open the door, and Jace Kingston lifts his hands up to me. "Welcome to the neighborhood."

"Thanks, man. Come on in." I step aside and watch him put the cookies down, then take out two beers and offer me one.

"It's been a long time, man. Congratulations on the job."

I take the beer with a laugh. "News moves fast around here."

"If you think it moves fast in this town, you should see the speed of light it hits in my family." He clinks his beer with mine. "I was glad you took the job. You were my first pick when Max asked. Now I'm hoping the beers loosen you up, so I can be your first pick."

"Not following you, man." Jace is a solid decade older than me. But I've looked up to him. He was the first professional athlete I ever knew. But that was because I knew him before he was drafted. "I thought you were retired. You want back on the ice?"

"Nah, man. My wife would have my balls if I thought about playing again. One too many surgeries made sure that's not in the cards. But I'm fucking bored as shit. And I only know one thing. *Hockey*. I know it fucking well. And I know this *team* even better. Let me help you win the next Cup."

I look at Jace Kingston and wonder how this is my life.

When did I get to the point where one of the greatest guys to ever lace up a pair of skates is asking me for a job?

"I don't have final say. I've got to run it by Max and get his okay before I could bring you on, but I think you'd be a real asset to have on this team. Any issues with you and your brother I should know about? I mean, you could have gone directly to him, right?" I'm not sure of this family's dynamic yet, and don't want to fuck it all to hell on my first day as head coach if I can help it.

"Nah, man. Max and I are good. You'll like working with him. He's a great GM. But as someone who's played the game, I didn't want to go to the GM. I wanted to go to the coach. I know I was a damn good player. But I've never coached. I'll be low man on the totem pole. I don't want your job. But I want a job. I don't like not being part of the team. And it's your team now."

"Good answer. I can respect that."

Jace's grin grows. "Well, I'll let you get back to it. I promised my wife, Indy, I wouldn't be long. She and my daughter, Saylor, made the cookies. The boys wanted to come and meet you too. They weren't thrilled when I said not this time."

"Oh yeah? Little hockey players?" I ask, my curiosity piqued.

"Cohen isn't so little anymore. He turned seventeen last month, and fuck if he's not giving me a run for my money. He was pushing for the draft last year, and his mother and I want him to go to college. Max is loving my pain because he and I had the same fight at his age." He laughs with a shrug. "Saylor's twelve, and the twins are nine. How old's your daughter, Deacon?"

"Same age as your twins. She just turned nine. Looks like she's actually going to be moving in with me soon," I tell him, thinking maybe she could make a few friends. Maybe that will help her with the transition.

"We'll have to do a BBQ. A welcome to the neighborhood. Prepare for the shit show party," he tells me as he moves around the kitchen and throws out his beer. "I'm sure Indy will be all over it. She loves parties. Any reason to throw one makes her happy."

My doorbell rings, and we both look up.

Fuck. I doubt Brynlee wants her uncle to know she's here. Not yet.

"Well, I took up enough of your time. We'll talk soon." He shakes my hand.

"Yeah. Sounds good. Thanks for stopping by."

I wait until Jace lets himself out the back door before moving to the front door and letting Brynlee in. "Hey, beautiful."

She blushes sweetly and walks through the door, then drops her purse on the floor, and we both move.

BRYNLEE

Book the trip. Kiss the boy. Eat the chocolate. Dance in the rain. Make the memories. Stop being scared. Before you know it, your life will be over. You don't want to be filled with nothing but regrets.

—*Brynlee's Secret Thoughts*

I'm lifted in his arms, and my breath catches while my mind whirls.

Lord, I missed this man. This connection.

It's wild. It's unlike anything I've ever felt before.

The kiss is hot and heavy and somehow safe in a way I wasn't expecting.

Who am I kidding? I wasn't expecting any of this, but I'm desperate for more.

I'd say it's as easy as breathing, but this man takes my breath away.

And when I'm slowly lowered back down on suddenly

unsteady feet, I cling to Deacon's waist for balance and rest my forehead against his chest. "Hi," I whisper.

"Hi," he answers with lips pressed against the top of my head. "You just missed your uncle."

"Max?" I wonder aloud, without letting go of my hold just yet.

"No. Jace."

"What?" My head pops up and nails Deacon in the chin.

Shit.

"Sorry." I press a kiss to his chin as my cheeks heat with embarrassment, then grab my bag from the floor.

"You're gonna have to hit me harder than that to make it hurt, red." Laughter dances in his dark blue eyes, and he presses a hand to the small of my back, moving me through the gorgeous house I haven't been in, in a few years.

"Hey," I tease as we walk into the kitchen. "Meet me in the cage, and I'll show you just how hard I can hit."

"Noted." He grabs two steaks from the counter and opens the back door. "I probably should have asked if you eat steaks."

"I do eat steak. Can I help with anything?" I pull a bottle of wine from my bag and set it on the counter, then move across the room. "And don't think you've gotten out of explaining what the hell Jace was doing here."

He pulls a salad from the fridge and motions to the pantry. "Just pick a dressing. I'm going to grill the steak and potatoes."

I pick two dressings out, not sure which he wants, then find two wine glasses and a bottle opener and follow Deacon outside. The view of the lake looks a little different from here than it did just a few weeks ago.

Holy. Hell.

Was it really just a few weeks ago?

I somehow feel like I've known him so much longer than that.

With a quiet hum deep in my throat, I watch him at the grill and enjoy the way his muscles move beneath his shirt. From a purely professional perspective, of course. I hand him a glass of wine and sit down at the table, crossing my legs and enjoying the lose flow of my sundress over my bare knees. "Okay, spill. What was Jace doing here?"

Deacon gets everything situated, then sits next to me at the table and sips his wine.

No man should look this good. It's truly unfair.

"This needs to stay between us, okay?"

"Ooh, now I'm intrigued." I lean in conspiratorially and smile when he cocks his head, waiting patiently for me to agree. "Yeah, yeah. Fine. My lips are sealed."

When a filthy smile stretches across lips that spent an entire night worshipping my body, heat pools in my stomach. "Get your mind out of the gutter, Kane."

"I'll see what I can do, St. James."

"Focus, Deacon. Why was Jace here, and are you expecting any more of my family to unexpectedly drop by anytime soon? Because I'd like to keep whatever this is between us for a while before the Kingston horde descends."

"The Kingston horde?" he questions, and I take another sip of my favorite red wine.

"Trust me. It's fitting," I warn.

"Jace wants a job," he finally fesses up.

"Shut. Up. Jace Kingston asked you for a job? Oh my God. Lindy is going to die."

"Lindy?"

"Yes, Lindy. When she married your goalie the season before last, Jace gave her and Easton so much shit. And then he went and retired at the end of the season. She's not gonna believe it when he comes back."

"Cone of silence, Brynlee," he warns, and I mime zipping my lips, but Deacon shakes his head and gets up to flip the steaks.

I think I kinda like that he already knows some of my fucked up family dynamic. Dating has never been an easy thing for me. The Kingston name comes with a ton of baggage, and I'm lucky enough to also be a St. James, which comes with its own unique challenges. Like finding a guy who isn't trying to date me to meet my father, or fuck me to screw over my father, or isn't so damn scared of my father that he won't even ask me out in the first place.

It's a bitch, if I'm being honest.

But sitting here with Deacon, I think it may have been worth wading through the others if they led me here.

While Deacon finishes grilling the steaks, I make myself at home in his kitchen and find the plates and utensils, then bring them and the salad outside and set the table. As he brings the steak and potatoes over, then gets the wine and refills our glasses, I decide, without a shadow of a doubt, this is the best first date I've ever had.

I mean . . . I guess technically our night on the beach was our first date.

But was it?

It feels like that first night somehow never ended.

I can't figure it out, and I'm not sure I care or want to.

It just feels right.

Which makes even less sense.

"So . . ." Needing to get out of this upside-down spiral, I change the subject. "Do you want to talk about what's happening with Isla?"

Deacon leans back in his chair and looks out at the lake. "Well, you know she asked if I would take full custody of Kennedy for the next two years. We haven't settled on a nanny yet, and oh yeah, she also assumed you and I were serious, and you being there as a constant in Kennedy's life was a big bonus for her."

"Oh . . ." I'm not really sure what else to say.

I want to ask him if he liked the sound of that.

I want to know if that scared him.

Hell . . . does it scare me?

Should it?

Or is this my one chance at a family I might not get otherwise?

"She wants us all to do a family dinner this weekend, so Kennedy can get to know you." His voice is pained, and there are so many warning flares that go off between that sentence and that look, I'm not sure which to dodge first.

And that thought hits me harder than any strike in any octagon ever has.

But that's the thing . . . My gut has always told me when to dodge a hit. Dad likes to say it's in our genes. Killian and I say it's because we had a good teacher. Either way, I know when to dodge, and I know when to plant my feet and fight. And I'm thinking right now may be one of the times I need to wade into the fight.

"What do you want, Deacon?"

He finally drags his gaze away from the lake, and when he looks at me, I recognize the weight he's carrying.

I've been walking around with it for weeks.

Different reasons.

Same weight.

"Here's the thing . . . Kennedy is the most amazing kid in the world. Her heart is huge. I'm not allowed to kill a spider in front of her or she cries, this kid has such a big heart. But she deals with anxiety. Always has. She's not big on change and generally hates meeting new people. It all makes her uncomfortable, and when she's uncomfortable, she shuts down."

"Poor kid. I can't imagine she'd love moving to a new country with a new language and new customs." What I leave unsaid is I can't imagine it could possibly be easy for her to move into her father's house and start a new school either. Add a stranger into the mix, and I might just make things worse—not better.

"No, that wouldn't be good for her. I'm worried about how hard my schedule will be on her. Isla and I already can't even agree on a nanny to interview, let alone hire. I'm worried. I don't want to give Isla any reason to think that taking Kennedy to Japan is the answer." He rubs his jaw and looks away again. "I've already missed so much of her life, I don't want to miss anymore. But I also don't want to pass up this opportunity with the Revolution."

He finally looks at me, and I almost wish he hadn't, his pain is so evident in every line of his face. "When I got hurt, I thought I'd never love another job the way I loved being a hockey player. Watching a dream slip through your fingers without having any control over it is a fucking bitch. But I didn't dwell. I rehabbed as best I could and came up with a new dream. A different dream. Coaching was never what I saw when I looked into my future, but I'm damn good at it. And now I fucking love it. And getting this chance . . . it's my one chance. If I don't take it, it's not going to come around again. I feel like I'm in a no-win situation."

My heart hurts for Deacon.

"I already told you, you can't turn down this job. Not now. You've already signed the contract, and this job is perfect for you." My heart pounds wildly inside my chest.

I can't imagine being in this position.

Having to make this impossible decision.

Maybe that's why I do what I'm about to do.

"Do you know that my mom isn't my biological mom?" I

ask hesitantly, unable to wrap my head around my train of thought.

"No, I didn't. Scarlet's not your mother?" His words aren't meant to be cruel, but I bristle a little anyway.

"She's not my biological mother. *That woman* . . ." I choose my words very carefully. "She was never a part of my life. She actually died recently, and I wasn't even told until her parents reached out to Dad a few weeks later."

I drop my hands into my lap and clasp my fingers together until the blood stops flowing

and my racing heart slows. "Dad and Scarlet dated in high school and reconnected when I was three. Scarlet Kingston has been my mother every day since. But if it weren't for my aunts being there before that, my life before Scarlet would have looked very different."

"I'm not really following you, Brynn." It's not just the sound of my name on his lips or the pain in his voice that has my mind working overtime. But those things, together with my inner voice saying maybe . . . *just maybe* this will be the only chance at a family I might ever get, are what I'll say caused my momentary insanity when I'm asked later.

And I'm going to be asked because this is crazy.

But, hey, so far everything about Deacon and me has felt crazy.

"I'm your answer, Deacon. Marry me," I tell him with as much confidence as I can muster.

"Brynlee . . ."

"Hear me out. I'm not saying I'm in love with you. I've had blowouts that lasted longer than the amount of time we've known each other."

"That's not true," he argues gently.

"Close enough. I'm not the same person I was as a kid, and neither are you. But that's fine. That's not why this will work. This works because I'll be done with the Revolution before you ever have to travel out of town for a single night. I'll be here. I can stay with Kennedy. I'm not saying as her mom, but family comes in a lot of forms. And I can be her family. Bonus points, that would give me legal rights if you're across the country and her mother is in another hemisphere." *Holy shit.* I can't believe I managed to hide the tremble in my voice. "She'll have to get used to the first big change, but then, there wouldn't be another."

"That's a huge change, Brynn. I mean, just looking at it from a father's perspective, Kennedy is already going to deal with the change of living with me and of a new school. Now you want to throw a wife into the mix?" he asks without any venom in his voice. Just concern, and concern I can understand.

"Isn't that basically what you're looking to do with a nanny?" I question. "At least with me I'm not being paid to be here. I'm someone she could count on. I'm someone who could care about her."

Deacon sits across from me, shell-shocked. "Why . . . why would you offer to put your life on hold, Brynn? Why would you do this for me? What could you possibly get out of this? You're young and smart and beautiful. You have a great family. Why would you tie yourself down with my mess."

"Why not. Deacon? None of us are promised tomorrow. I could be dead before I turn twenty-five—"

"Fucking hell, Brynlee. Don't say that." He moves next to me, radiating a sexy protective possessiveness that scares me. I don't want to break this man.

"Deacon, there's some—"

"And what if it doesn't work out? We just cut ties and go our separate ways? I work for your family, red. I'm not sure that's going to be as clean as it sounds." His hand cups my face, while his dark eyes stare at me like they're trying desperately to understand me. "And what about your family?"

"We'd deal with them after we worked it out with Isla and Kennedy."

Deacon stares at me for so long, I start to wonder if he's shocked into silence.

Was this the stupidest thing I've ever done?

But just when I think maybe I should take it all back, he pulls me up in front of him and holds my face gently in both hands. "You'd really do this for me?"

"I would," I answer, savoring his warmth against my skin. "But Deacon, there are things—"

"It would need to be fast," he cuts me off before I get a chance to say more, lost in his own thoughts. "Like before Isla leaves."

I nod, understanding what he's saying. His ex-wife is leaving in a week.

I close my eyes, and words sit on the tip of my tongue until I can work up the courage to say them. "Would you think I was crazy if I said I have a friend who's a judge who owes me a favor?" I laugh nervously because why stop sounding like a lunatic now? "I taught her self-defense one-on-one a few years ago. She told me if I ever needed anything, I just needed to ask."

The smile that pulls across his handsome face is everything. "Baby, I think we're both crazy because I'd ask if she could stop by tonight."

"Wait—" I stop us. "Can we keep this quiet until I'm done working for the Revolution? I've worked hard for my professional reputation, and I'd rather people find out after the fact. Like once I'm working for Crucible. "

"That's in a week, right?"

I nod, butterflies taking flight in my stomach.

"What would we tell Kennedy?" He runs his fingers

through my hair and tugs before they trail over my bare arms.

"What if we tell her the truth if she asks.? Well . . . a very curated version of it. We couldn't wait to get married, so we didn't. But I'm switching jobs, and we're both high-profile people, so we decided to keep things quiet for the next week."

"And you'd move in once you switch jobs?" Deacon's eyes flare and heat, and I find myself straddling the line of wanting him to fuck me senseless and wanting to sit down and figure everything out.

I nod and rest my hands under his shirt, right above his belt, needing to feel his skin under my hands.

"Call your judge, Brynlee," he growls, and every single inch of my body stands at attention.

"Yes, Coach." I smile.

"Oh, baby, we can play with that later."

"Oh, I like that. Better yet . . ."—I run my teeth over my lip—"husband."

BRYNLEE

I wasn't nervous when I basically proposed to my now husband.

I was no blushing bride when I called in my favor and said my vows in a ceremony that lasted less than five minutes. Even my friend explaining how she was going to handle our marriage license Monday and me thanking her *again* for pulling all sorts of strings didn't make me hesitate. But now, standing at the edge of the lake and staring into the light show the fireflies are putting on for me while Deacon escorts Judge Guiliano out, I'm left with a rapidly racing mind I can't silence.

I just promised myself to a man who barely knows me and certainly doesn't know the complicated future I could be looking at. And that thought alone gives me my first small niggling of doubt.

Soft footsteps fall in the damp grass behind me, but I don't turn.

I don't need to.

I can already tell it's Deacon from the cadence of his steps. He walks with purpose. *Always*. And after spending just a few short nights with him, I already know this man doesn't believe in wasting time in any aspect of his life.

I guess that worked in his favor tonight.

Strong arms wrap around me from behind, and he rests his chin on my head. "How are you feeling, red?"

His words are soft and serious, and my heart pangs in response.

"Like a woman who just got married without any of the fuss or stress of a wedding." I wrap my arms around his and lean back into the safety of his chest. "I feel strangely . . . *free*. Which makes absolutely no sense."

"You are free. You run this show. You make the rules," he soothes my slowly fraying nerves.

I turn in his arms and press my palms against his chest, enjoying the weight of his hands on me. "What if I don't want this to be a show?"

"I'm not following you." He runs a hand over my hair, tucking a lock behind my ear, and I'm struck by just how hard I'm already falling for this man.

"I guess what I mean is . . . I know this marriage is for show. At least it will be once we can tell people. But you and me . . . I want us to be real with each other. I want us to be honest. I think what I'm trying to say is I don't want it all to be a lie."

"It's not all a lie, Brynn. We're not a lie," he attempts to reassure me.

"But how can you be so sure?" I ask, unable to settle the thoughts in my head.

"Because a lie wouldn't feel like this." Deacon's eyes flare. "I think it's time I take you upstairs and reassure you just how much I want my wife." Before I can argue with him, he throws me over his shoulder in a fireman's carry and slaps my ass as his long legs quickly eat up the distance to the house.

"You cannot carry me up those stairs . . ." I argue, staring up at the huge wooden staircase, but this man isn't listening.

"Like fuck I can't." He takes the steps two at a time, then kicks his bedroom door open and tosses me to the bed like a rag doll.

I bounce with a laugh and try to catch my bearings. "You're crazy . . ."

"No, baby. You're the crazy one. But I fucking love it. Now strip." He pulls his shirt over his head and drops it to the floor before I can move.

I'm lost in the perfection that is my new husband's chest. Like a golden god, each tanned beautiful muscle is carved to perfection from his pecs to his abs down to the mouthwatering V of his obliques. "Now let me see what's under that dress, red." His pupils blow wide with want, and my fears start to subside. "Did you wear pretty panties for me?"

"Maybe," I taunt without moving. This man has no clue how vast my lingerie collection is, and I think I'm going to have fun teasing him with it. This could be fun.

"Show me," he demands, and it's so fucking hot.

Who knew I'd like a bossy man?

He stalks toward the bed, eyes locked on mine, and runs his tongue over his lip, hungry, and my God, his hunger is such a turn-on. Long, rough fingers skim over the bare skin on my shoulder and under the strap of my sundress when he says, "Were you thinking about me . . ."— his gaze rakes over me, lingering on my mouth for a beat too long before he swallows—"when you got dressed? Did you think about how it would feel when I peeled your clothes off you?"

Both straps are slid down my arms, and I nod, breathless.

Utterly incapable of forming a coherent thought.

"Words, wife. I want to hear you."

Deacon

Brynlee sits on her knees on the bed, her gorgeous green eyes glazed with need as her delicate fingers play with her top button, and without thinking, I reach for her. Desperate to taste her skin, but my girl slaps my hands away instead.

She pops open the top button on her black linen sundress, then the next one and the next until a scrap of green lace—so dark it rivals the color of her eyes—peeks past the hem. My mouth waters. "I thought of you," she finally whispers, and her words go right to my already-hard cock.

"Tell me . . ." I move closer but don't touch this time. Not yet.

"About whether you'd like lace or silk," she adds as her hands slide down to the belt tied at her waist. "If you'd like French cut or thong."

Fucking hell, she's killing me.

Her hands slide inside the dress, pushing it down until it pools at her feet, and she's left standing in front of me like a goddess. Dark green lace shimmers against her pale skin, giving teasing glimpses of the forbidden. The hint of a pale pink nipple. The outline of a bare pussy. The damp spot between her legs. "I wondered whether you'd like what you see."

I step forward without words and watch, a man balancing on a tightrope as Brynlee presses her hot lips to the base of my throat. *Fuck*. It's like she's struck a match, and we're both watching it burn down, waiting to see who gives in first.

"Brynnlee . . ." I growl in warning, unsure how much more I can take.

She presses another kiss against my skin before ghosting her lips over mine.

"Our marriage might not be real, Deacon, but I need us to be. *Please* . . ." she pleads, and any control I thought I had disappears along with all the oxygen in the room.

Swallowed whole by the fire.

Slowly . . . I move so goddamn slowly . . . slow enough that I can commit every inch of this woman's body to my memory—so years from now when I'm old, and no doubt alone, I'll still remember this woman and this night. I slide my hands over her ribs and under her breasts before dragging her closer, needing to feel her against me. Wanting to take my time. To savor her.

She moves closer with each slide of skin on skin.

Each touch, until I bend my knees and cup her face in my hands, bringing us eye to eye. "*We* are real, red. Nothing has ever been this real. Fuck everyone else."

She ghosts her lips over mine with a smile. "I'd rather fuck *you*, Deacon."

"Crazy girl," I growl against her mouth. "Tonight, we take our time," I promise her before my tongue slides against hers. Teasing her. I want to learn every way there is that makes this woman melt. All the ways to coax that sexy sigh out of her again . . . and again. Every place to kiss. To suck. To bite. I want to earn all her pleasure, so I can own all her orgasms.

The air around us is charged like an electrical storm.

You know the destruction it brings will be massive, but the beauty that comes first is worth the pain.

Our mouths crash together, like a heavy clap of thunder, and I wrap a hand around her head and fist her long hair, deepening our kiss. Controlling it. Running my teeth over her soft lips, swallowing her sighs, and sliding my tongue against hers.

Desperate for this woman who just gave me a piece of herself I didn't deserve.

This woman who can't possibly understand what she just gave me.

Brynn pulls her mouth away, panting as her nails score my skin, branding me, and fuck that's a turn-on. I want her brand. She drags her tongue down the column of my neck and over my pulse as she reaches down and unbuckles my belt and pants.

"Brynn . . ." I warn as my last fraying strand of restraint threatens to finally snap.

She presses her lips to my chest, just over my heart, then pushes me back and slips off the bed to her knees, dragging my zipper down.

Damn . . . the wicked smile kissing her lips is fucking gorgeous.

"You gonna be a good girl and take my dick out, *wife?*"

Her eyes widen, and she cocks her head to the side, regarding me. "Is that a question or a command, husband?" Her long lashes flutter, and swear to God, a man could forget his own name looking at Brynlee St. James on her knees. "Because I kinda like it when you get controlling, but I think I want to see *you* lose control even more."

"You haven't seen controlling yet, Brynlee."

She smiles so fucking sweetly, I almost miss the pink that floods her cheeks.

With shaking hands, she shoves my boxer briefs down and *tries* to wrap her fist around my dick.

And when she finally drags her tongue from the base of my cock up to the tip, I give in to the urge I've had since that very first night on the beach and wrap her soft, strawberry-blonde hair around my fist and tug.

Brynn moans, and something cracks in my chest. I fucking love that sound.

My spine snaps tight when those pretty pink lips wrap around my cock. Her eyes water, and she hums deep in her chest, then swallows me down her throat, and I'm fucking done for.

This gorgeous woman on her knees is going to be my undoing.

"Brynn . . ." I growl when my dick hits the back of her throat. "Fuck, baby."

I lift her up and swallow her protest as I lie her on the bed and climb between her legs, fucking desperate for her. "Condom?" I ask with one shaky word, every inch of me strung tight.

"I wasn't done," she pouts.

"Brynlee—" I warn, any semblance of control gone. Shredded at her feet.

"No." She wraps her legs around my waist and drags her nails down my back. "No condom." A hum builds deep in her throat as she arches her back and rubs her chest against mine.

This woman was made for me. Every soft curve fits perfectly against the hard planes of my body.

Fucking perfect.

Fucking mine.

"Please . . . Deacon." She wraps her arms around my neck, and her tongue meets mine, stroke for stroke. Begging for more with each shaky breath.

I roll us so Brynn straddles me. Her red hair spills softly around pale shoulders tinged pink from a hint of sun. She trembles above me when I drag my tongue along one of her flawless fucking tits—perfect handfuls with pretty pink nipples begging to be sucked.

Her green eyes sparkle as she lifts up on her knees and

fists one hand around my cock. She fits me against her hot, wet pussy, then lowers herself down. *Slowly.* Teasing us both. Taking me inch by slower inch into her tight cunt until I'm filling her completely.

She moans and presses one palm against my chest for leverage as she watches us.

Watches me as I slide inside her.

So fucking tight.

So fucking hot.

I slide my hands over her thighs, my fingertips biting into her soft skin. "You take my cock like such a good girl. Now show me how much you like it, baby."

Those emerald-green eyes close, and her mouth opens on a silent sob. "You've got to give me a second, Deacon . . ." She inhales a shaky, stuttered breath as her body relaxes, stretching to accommodate me. "It's too much."

I wrap an arm around her waist and jackknife up, holding her even closer. Breathing her in each time she breathes out. Wide eyes hold mine as I slowly fuck her.

"You're fucking perfect, wife." My tongue traces her bottom lip before I tug it between my teeth. "My fucking wife."

Her shoulders shake, and she wraps her arms around my neck, clinging to me as the electricity humming around us threatens to destroy us both.

"None of this makes sense, Deacon." She traces her lips around my ear, then bites down. "But I am yours. For as long as we do this, I'm yours. Only yours."

An overwhelming, possessive need roars through me, and the final string snaps.

My composure is completely eviscerated.

"I can't be gentle, Brynn," I tell her, knowing this woman already owns me.

"Then don't be and don't stop," she whispers against my lips.

"Fuck, red . . ." I drive up into her over and over, swallowing her moans and holding her impossibly close. We move together against each other. Finding a punishing rhythm.

Pushing us higher and higher until she's a trembling, sobbing, beautiful mess.

Begging and pleading.

Moaning into my mouth.

Nothing has ever sounded better. Tasted better. Nothing.

"Gonna need you to come for me, baby," I growl against her mouth and circle her clit with my fingers just before a beautiful sound rips from her throat.

"Deacon. Oh my God. Yes . . . please. *God*," she cries out as shudders rack her beautiful body.

I slow my thrusts, fucking her through her endless orgasm, dragging it out until I'm kissing away her tears as she lies limp, draped in my arms.

But I'm not done.

Not yet. Not ever.

I pull out, and her eyes glaze over as her cum drips down my dick.

"Give me one more, baby," I tell her before pushing back into her drenched, swollen pussy.

"Jesus, Deacon . . ." she whimpers as her eyes try to focus.

If someone had told me ten years ago that this would be the woman who would destroy me, I wouldn't have believed them.

Now I wonder how I fucking missed it all those years ago.

I thrust into her slowly. Achingly slow.

Fucking my wife until she's left without any doubt of just how real she and I are.

Until it's just us.

Until Brynlee is right here with me.

Moaning with every snap of my hips.

I want my wife to feel me between her legs for fucking days.

Red-hot heat tugs at the base of my spine as my heart thunders in my chest, and I come on a roar as she splinters and shatters beneath me.

One word whispered over and over in my mind.

Mine.

The Philly Press

KROYDON KRONICLES

SWOONY & SINGLE

Hey, hey, all you beautiful people. I have it on good authority that the Philadelphia Revolution has officially hired it's youngest, hottest, head coach in franchise history. Deacon Kane, hailing all the way from Boston University, has been stolen away by Philly's favorite hockey team. And let me tell you something, this man is definitely another hockey hottie to add to our Puck Pack. Rumor is he's a single dad too, ladies. I feel a new hashtag is in order.

#SwoonyandSingle #PuckPack #HockeyHottie #KroydonKronicles

DEACON

I roll over and reach for Brynlee to pull her against me, but cold, empty sheets meet my touch instead of my warm, willing *wife*.

Fuck... *my wife*.

I'm not sure that's something I thought I'd say again in my life, but there's something about it that causes a visceral reaction somewhere deep in my soul that makes no fucking sense.

I reach over to catch the time on my phone but see a missed text from Brynlee instead.

> **BRYNLEE**
> Looks like our secret is safe, husband. The Kroydon Kronicles is running with a story about you being named head coach. They don't even realize it was probably leaked by the Revolution on purpose.

> **DEACON**
> You snuck out without saying goodbye, wife.

BRYNLEE

Nope. I said goodbye and kissed you too. You tried to tug me back down, but I had to get home and get changed. I have a player coming into the office this morning.

DEACON

Who?

BRYNLEE

Who . . . Do you mean which player has an appointment?

DEACON

I mean what man did you leave our bed for?

BRYNLEE

Daniels.

I run through my mental checklist of the team roster until I place Daniels. He's a few years older than me with a wife and three daughters. But he's still going to be skating the boards until he pukes for the entire first week of practice because he's the poor fuck who pulled Brynlee out of my bed this morning.

DEACON

I thought you were off today.

BRYNLEE

I was, but he messaged me yesterday and asked if I could help him today. Then I promised my mom I'd meet her for coffee. After that, I have to pick up Winnie from Gracie. I promise I'll be back before Isla and Kennedy get there.

DEACON

Your bringing Winnie to my house?

BRYNLEE

Yeah. I thought she might help with Kennedy. And before you say it, I'm well aware I'm using my dog to get your daughter to like me.

Shit. Does she like dogs?

My crazy girl.

DEACON

Yeah, red. She likes dogs. Do you need me to order anything for Winnie?

BRYNLEE

Nope. I've got everything I need. She's a very portable puppy. Just don't leave your shoes lying around. She's teething.

DEACON

Whatever you say, wife.

BRYNLEE

See you soon.

BRYNLEE

When life gives you lemons, trade them for coffee beans. Who the fuck drinks lemonade anyway?

—Brynlee's Secret Thoughts

I dart through the rain into Sweet Temptations to meet my mother later that day, then thank whatever deity could possibly exist that she's nowhere to be seen when I get there. Aunt Amelia is behind the bake case, stacking fresh chocolate-chip cookies, and the delicious scent of crème brûlée coffee draws me in like a wizard casting a spell.

If coffee is a love language, my translation is vanilla bean and burnt sugar.

Amelia smiles and hands me a cookie before she pours my coffee without bothering to ask what I want. She already knows. It hasn't changed in years. "Here you go, Brynnie."

"Thank you." I take my first sip and let it work its magic.

"Looks like your mom just parked outside."

"Don't look so surprised, Aunt Amelia," I mock that she's at all surprised to see Mom getting out of her Maybach.

Why would she be?

The Kingston family phone tree might be as bad and fast as the internet.

Who needs social media when you've got my family?

You can find out anything you ever wanted to know about anyone in this family with one or two well-placed phone calls. I'm sure everyone knows I quit by now. And knowing my mom, she's worked her flawless PR skills and spun it to make her look like the good guy.

Amelia laughs and wipes down the counter, then makes Mom's coffee and plates two more cookies. "Be nice to your mom, Brynn. She means well."

I roll my eyes like a sullen teenager and take our coffee and sweets over to the table in the farthest corner of the shop. We're not getting privacy here, but since I refused to come to the house, this was as neutral of a spot as we were getting. I'm not even sure how many come-to-Jesus meetings we've all had here at Sweet Temptations.

Break up with a boy, meet your friends here to drown your sorrows in cupcakes.

Only have a few minutes to catch up with the girls? Great. Everyone meet for coffee because we were all going to be drinking it anyway.

The entire family is pissing you off? Okay. Meet at Aunt Amelia's shop because she's the only sister everyone listens to.

Mom shakes out her umbrella and leans it against the table as she drops a kiss on my head. "Hi, honey."

"Hi," I offer, still way too pissed to be having this discussion. Any discussion, really.

I push her coffee across the table and sip mine in silence.

THE SWEET SPOT

"Brynlee ... you can't be mad at me."

"Oh. That's your first mistake, Mom. I can, and I am." I make sure to keep my voice controlled and soft. I refuse to make a scene, and at this point, there's nothing she can say that will change my mind. "I'll get over it, but I'm not there yet. I know you think the world has to bend to the timeframe of Scarlet Kingston-St. James, but I hate to break it to you ... That doesn't include your children. We learned to tell you no years ago."

Mom sips her coffee and crosses her long legs. She may not be my biological mother, but ironically, we look a lot alike. Though, unfortunately for me, everyone else in my family—including my mother—were all blessed with long legs. Everyone but me, that is.

"Honey, I was just trying to look out for you. The Kings travel less than the Revolution, and their season is shorter. It would be easier on your body." She reaches across the table to rest her hand on mine, but I pull it back.

Fate is a cruel bitch.

For most of my life, I forgot Scarlet isn't my biological mom. She was the most amazing mother. She never treated me differently than Killian or Olivia. She still doesn't. Whenever someone else would bring it up, it would catch me off guard because it honestly wasn't something I ever thought about. My biological mom wasn't a good person, and I rarely ever thought about her.

But now ... now she's all I can think about.

Now she's all my parents see when they look at me.

Even dead, she's still coming up with a new way to ruin my life.

"I didn't ask for a new job, Mom. You wouldn't have done that for any other staff member—"

"You aren't just a staff member, Brynn. You're my daughter. Show me a parent who wouldn't move heaven and earth for their child, and I'll show you a bad parent." She sits perfectly straight with posture that would rival the Queen of England's, but it's a show. She's holding back tears. I know her tell. And damn her for making me feel bad because I'm not done being right just yet.

I dig my heels in just a little harder.

"I'm not a child anymore, Mom. You can't just mess with my job and my future because you think you know best."

And just like that, any tears she may have been fighting back die, and anger takes over.

"At least I'm trying to plan for your future. Someone has to. You're living like a flamingo with your head stuck in the sand, Brynlee. You're in limbo. You can't keep doing this."

Fire burns in the pit of my stomach.

"This is why—" I stop myself and choose my next words very carefully. "That kind of thinking is why I am not ready to make any decisions yet. My head isn't stuck in the sand. I'm living my life. I'm enjoying it. Hell, Mom, I'm thriving. I'm also counting down the days until I'm no longer under the umbrella of King Corp. so I don't have to worry about you trying to manage my life for me because you don't approve of my decisions." I stand and take my coffee with me.

"Oh, honey," she chides softly. "Someone has to manage your life since you refuse to do it."

"I love you so much, Mom. And I know you *think* you're doing the right thing. But instead of letting me make my own choices for my own life, you're trying to force your choices onto me. If someone had done that to you at my age, you would have burned the city of Philadelphia to the ground just to prove them wrong." I bend down and kiss her cheek. "You've never been a hypocrite before. Don't be one now."

And with that, I leave her behind and run through the rain to my car.

I think about trying to call Kenzie, but I doubt she'll be able to talk. Across the street, Lindy and Everly's bridal gown shop is open, and they're probably both in there, but stopping by right now doesn't even make sense. For the first time in my life, I'm keeping things from all my friends, and the worst part is I'm not sure I'm ready to change any of it.

"You look pretty," Gracie leans her head against the bathroom door and looks me over. "Where are you going?"

"I'm in a bra and panties, Gracie. I look like a stripper," I argue as I get ready for my big dinner with Deacon's family, wishing I could tell her more, but she and I are continuing our own version of *don't ask, don't tell*, and tonight isn't the night to break that truce.

Grace moves next to me and runs her fingers through the soft waves of my hair that refused to be tamed. I can relax the curls, but the waves will never be gone. "Fine," she sighs before boosting herself up on my bathroom counter. "How was coffee with your mom?"

Now it's my turn to sigh, already over today and trying to put on a good face for tonight. "She's frustrated because I won't do what she wants, and I'm frustrated because she thought it was okay to play puppet master with my life."

"How come no one ever told us how much our twenties would kick our asses?" Gracie looks down at her foot, and I know what she's thinking. She's a ballerina at the height of her career, and she's battling an injury and battling herself right now while she figures out what her next move is.

The move is easy for me to see, but I'm looking at it from

the outside. It's harder when it's your life and you're left to make the hard choices. I should know. I've been avoiding certain choices all summer.

I slip a white sundress dotted with tiny green flowers over my head and adjust the ties on my shoulders, then look at one of my oldest friends. "If they had told us, we wouldn't have believed them."

She shrugs one shoulder up to her chin and side-eyes me carefully. "Wear your emerald earrings . . . the ones set in the little diamond circles. They'll make the green in your eyes and the green in the dress pop."

I walk into my room with Gracie on my heels and lace up a pair of brown chunky-heeled sandals, then grab the earrings my dad gave me for my twenty-first birthday.

"Don't hold a grudge against your mom for too long, Brynnie. Maybe she's just trying to tell you something you don't want to believe." She wiggles her fingers at me in a wave. "I'm heading out. Have fun tonight."

"Thanks, Grace." I watch her leave as a pit begins to form in my stomach.

How many secrets can I juggle at once before everything comes crashing down?

I get Winnie strapped into her car seat in the back of my car and stare at my Bluetooth screen. One message wouldn't be the end of the world. Fuck it.

BRYNLEE

I did something.

> **KENZIE**
> Well hello to you too.

> **BRYNLEE**
> Don't give me shit. It's not like you have time for small talk. You keep telling me how busy you are.

> **KENZIE**
> I'm lying in the break room, supposed to be catching a few minutes of sleep while I can. But my brain won't slow down. Wanna text or talk?

> **BRYNLEE**
> FaceTime?

> **KENZIE**
> **Thumbs up emoji**

My phone rings as the emoji hits my screen, and I brace myself. "Hey," I answer as Kenzie pops up in pink scrubs. "You look good," I lie.

"Shut up. I look like I haven't slept in a week and was knee-deep in amniotic fluid forty minutes ago while I delivered the biggest baby I've ever caught." She holds the phone above her face, lying back on a pillow in a dark room.

"It still sounds strange," I mumble.

"Listen, it's what we do. We catch babies." Kenzie wasn't lying. Bags big enough to move states line her eyes, and even in the dark on-call room, I can tell she hasn't seen the sun in days. Winnie's snores get louder from the back seat and Kenzie cracks up. "Tell my niece that Auntie Kenzie can't wait to meet the sleepy little potato."

"I will," I smile.

"That's not why you called, Brynnie. Now tell me what's

going on? What did you do?" she asks, very matter-of-factly, and I hesitate.

Am I really going to tell her this?

She groans when I don't answer right away.

"Brynnie... I'm supposed to be sleeping." Her words may seem irritated, but I know better. "Did you take the test?"

I look away from the screen and make sure there isn't anyone anywhere near my car in our parking garage. "No." When I lose the nerve I had a minute ago, I pivot instead of telling her about Deacon. "I yelled at Gracie this week. She's not listening to her body, and she's never going to get healthy and dance again unless she does."

Kenzie's eyes narrow on me, but she goes with it and doesn't call me out on my half-truth. "Do you want me to call her?"

I shake my head. "Not yet. But if I need you to, I promise I'll call."

"You sure nothing else is going on?" She pushes me because she knows there's more.

That's the problem with having a group of friends who know each other as well as we all do. We call you on your bullshit. And Kenzie—well, let's just say having your cousin as one of your best friends makes her uniquely qualified to push when the shit you're slinging starts to smell. I crinkle my nose with that incredibly disgusting thought and stare through my windshield.

"You have to promise you won't tell a soul—"

"I won't," she cuts me off, then sits up. "Brynnie... you're scaring me."

"Not even the girls," I warn her.

"Not a soul. I promise."

She won't. Kenzie has always had my back.

"I did something crazy last night." My cheeks heat, and

my stomach knots, but I can't stop the smile from forming anyway.

"And..." she pushes.

"And it's quite possibly the dumbest thing I've ever done..." A soft laugh slips past my lips. "I'd be scared if I woke up this morning with even an ounce of regret. But I didn't. And I guess I'm struggling with that."

She nods thoughtfully, like she's taking it all in, even though nothing I just said makes sense. "You're not going to tell me, are you?"

"I don't think I can yet," I admit, and there goes my stomach twisting again.

"Promise to tell me if you're in trouble, Brynn?"

"Always. But for now, I think I kind of just wanted someone to know."

She looks at something and groans. "Shit, B. I've got to go. Have I told you how much I hate full moons?"

"Love you, Kenz."

"You too, Brynnie. And B..." She waits while I stare at her. "Take the damn test. Gotta go. Bye."

I wait until the screen goes black, then whisper, "Bye."

DEACON

"You gotta relax, brother. It'll be fine. Isla's going to be her normal, extroverted self. She'll talk enough for everyone in the room. Even if Kennedy hates her new mommy, no one will notice."

"Remind me why the fuck we're friends?" I grumble and shove the meal I just had delivered into the warming drawer.

"Because if you hadn't blown me off at O'Malley's, you wouldn't have met your banging new wife. Seriously, have you seen the pictures of her modeling her dad's gym shirt and a green thong in some fashion show? Because brother, seriously, you outkicked your coverage. She's a fucking knockout."

"One more word and I'm going to kill you, Rip," I growl because, *yes*, I have seen the pictures online from a fashion show for the local lingerie shop a few years ago. And yes, I certainly did outkick my coverage. My wife is unbelievably gorgeous. But the idea that my best friend has seen her ass makes me see fucking red.

"Listen, would you rather I lied and said Kennedy was going to love her? Because she's not, and you know it.

Brynlee is new, and Kennedy doesn't do new. But your kid is moving in with you in one fucking week, Deacon. And your new wife is going to be what makes the whole machine keep running while you're traveling with the team. She'll keep Kennedy on a schedule. She won't be some nanny you have to worry about leaving my goddaughter with. And if you're lucky, she might let you touch her boobs when you get home."

"Jesus, Rip. Seriously?"

"Buddy, you're the one who married the girl last night. I wasn't expecting that news this morning. But you went for it, and it's actually genius. So warm up your food, stop your bitching, and make sure there's a room for me because I'm stopping by before the season starts, and I'm contractually obligated to kick your team's fucking ass." Rip laughs like the idea of beating my team is his new favorite goal in life, and I groan—*again*.

"You can try, asshole," I taunt. "See you in a few weeks."

"Later, Kane." Ripley ends the call, and I look around the empty house.

He's not wrong. Isla's going to be chattier than normal. It's what she does when she's nervous, and we're all nervous. This is a ton of fucking change for Kennedy. And what the hell am I supposed to do if my kid hates Brynlee?

As all the possible ways tonight can go to shit race through my mind, I hear the doorbell ring before it cracks open. "Honey ... I'm home."

Guess I forgot to lock the door.

I make a mental note to get her a key.

Not sure when the sound of her voice started to fucking center me, but that's exactly what it does. "I'm in the kitchen, *dear*," I tease as a tiny tornado runs ahead of Brynn into the kitchen and right into my leg. The little white and brown puppy lays its head on my foot and snorts, kinda like a piglet.

"What the hell, Brynn?"

She laughs sweetly and places two pink bakery boxes on the counter, then lifts up on her toes and wraps her arms around my neck. "Deacon, meet Winnie." Her citrusy scent is almost as mouthwatering as she is when she runs her lips over mine. "She's not the most energetic thing in the world. But she's a great bed buddy."

"I'm the only bed buddy you need, wife." I lift her up and sit her on the counter in front of me, then move between her legs and cup her face, forcing her eyes to mine. "How did this morning go with your mom?"

"You're going to be gone half the season. Winnie will be right here, keeping me and Kennedy company."

The fact she even thought to include my daughter in that sentence pulls at something deep in my fucking chest.

"And. . . my mom was her normal overbearing self. But that's her, and she's not going to change. Let's focus on your family tonight, okay? We'll have plenty of time to talk about my dysfunction later."

"You okay?" I ask, just before pressing my lips to her forehead. "This isn't one-way, you know? You're helping me. Let me help you."

She drops her hands to my chest and smiles. "Once I'm done with the Revolution and I tell my parents about you, there'll be plenty for you to deal with. Just be thankful Max is the Revolution's GM and not my mother."

"Hello . . ." Isla calls out as my front door opens.

"Knocking isn't optional, Mom," Kennedy lectures, and I smile.

Winnie's head lifts slowly from the floor, and she looks Brynlee's way but doesn't move. She's a cute, roly-poly little thing.

"You ready for this?" I ask Brynn as she shakes her head no. "Too late now, wife."

Kennedy is the first to walk into the kitchen, and she stops abruptly when she sees Brynn and me. Her body language is closed off. Lanky arms that she hasn't quite grown into yet are crossed over her chest as she glares at us. "Mom says it's rude to sit on the counter."

"Kennedy—" Isla chastises as Brynlee hops down.

"No, it's fine," Brynn reassures. "Your mom is right," she offers with a big beautiful smile. "Your dad is just so tall that it's easier to see his eyes if I cheat and gain a few inches."

Winnie picks that moment to realize new people have walked in the room, and she moves behind Brynn's leg, probably scared of the new people.

My daughter tilts her head to watch the chubby puppy.

"Who's that?" Kennedy questions, and I know she's talking about the dog, but I see my chance, and I take it.

I put my arm around Brynn and glance around the room at Kennedy, Isla, and Shaun. "Guys, this is Brynlee . . . My wife."

Brynlee

Well that was one way to share the news.

Deacon may be good at many, *many* things, but apparently tact isn't one of them.

"She meant the dog," I whisper, my eyes darting between Kennedy and Deacon.

Isla looks utterly shell-shocked, which is a complete one-eighty from the first time we met. "Oh my." She walks forward to hug Deacon, then turns to me. "Well you two certainly move fast."

Once she steps back, Shaun hands Deacon a case of beer and pats him on the back. "Congratulations, man. We're happy for you."

They both seem fine with our announcement. Kennedy, however, isn't saying a word. She blinks rapidly, looking between Deacon and me as the blood drains from her face.

Deacon reaches out, but she shrugs him away, careful not to let him touch her. She looks around the kitchen with tears rapidly filling her eyes and makes a beeline for the first exit she sees, letting the French doors slam shut with a deafening thud as she escapes into the backyard.

"Shit," Deacon murmurs as Winnie trots over to the glass door and watches Kennedy walk through the yard.

"Don't worry. It's just a lot for her right now," Isla reassures him without any weight behind her words. "Us moving, her moving . . . she was going to struggle with Brynlee no matter what you did. I just don't think any of us were expecting you two to get married quite so . . . *quickly*."

"It made sense," Deacon argues, and Isla takes a step back as if she's been slapped.

Then she wraps an arm around my shoulders. "Hope you weren't expecting romantic gestures and flowery words. That's not Deacon's way."

I know this is his ex-wife.

I know they're friends, and she's the mother of his child.

Obviously, I expected her to have a level of intimacy with this man.

My man . . .

But something about that statement just . . . I'm not sure I can pinpoint exactly what about it sets my hair on end, but it does. I've had enough people try to tell me what to expect today, and I've had my fill.

So I do what I do best.

I smile sweetly and remove myself from the situation but

not before getting the last word. "I don't need romantic words and flowers. There are plenty of other ways to express yourself, which Deacon happens to be very good at."

I slip out of her hold and scoop Winnie up in my arms, then move in front of my husband, who's cracked a small smile, thanks to my very loaded comment. "Would it be okay if I tried talking to her?"

"I'm not sure if that's the best move, Brynn." His smile vanishes, and tight lines take its place. "She usually needs time and space when she shuts down."

"Could I try?" I ask gently, not wanting this to be what sets the tone of my relationship with his daughter. "I won't push her. I promise."

"I think that would be nice, Brynlee." I turn to Isla, who surprises me with her answer. "Kennedy doesn't do well with new people, but maybe if she realizes that yes, you're new, but you're also permanent, it will help her begin to adjust."

Hesitantly, I lace my fingers through Deacon's and squeeze his hand in time with my heavy heartbeat. "Are you okay with this?"

"Give it a shot, fearless girl." He presses his lips to my forehead and runs his hand over Winnie's head. The trust he's showing warms me from the inside out. Even if he may never know just how full of fear I truly am.

The sun is shining, and the clouds have cleared when I make my way outside. A vast difference from this morning's summer storm. Humidity clings to the damp air, and I set Winnie down by the edge of the lake and snicker when she runs away from the water and glues herself to my leg.

Kennedy sits on the edge of the still-drying dock, her long legs dangle above the lake as the sun reflects off her shiny, nearly black hair. She's every bit her father's mini-me, but with her mother's striking golden-brown eyes, utterly beautiful, and in this moment, she looks painfully young and not at all prepared for the changes she's expected to navigate.

Without looking up, sadness and anxiety radiate off her in waves as I approach. My sandals creak with each step on the worn wooden planks, followed by quick clicking of Winnie's paws.

"Is this seat taken?" I ask as I carefully fold my sundress around my legs and sit down next to her. Close but careful not to get too close. Winnie plops between us, sandwiching herself halfway between each of our bodies, and I watch, somewhat in awe, as Kennedy digs her fingers into Winnie's soft fur and relaxes a tiny bit.

It's a tiny step, but I'll take anything.

Sad eyes appraise me silently before looking back out over the lake. Her hand stays on Winnie as we settle into a heavy silence for a long while.

A million memories of this lake run through my mind like an old home video.

Summer. BBQs. Nights spent telling ghost stories in front of a bonfire at Lindy's old house, and days spent at Uncle Jace's house, trying to get the cool uncle to sneak us a beer. Not that he ever did, but we always tried. At least until I tried my first beer and realized how disgusting they are. Pretty sure that was my first and last beer.

I turn my head away from her and look at the homes I can just barely make out through the tall trees that line the property between Deacon's and Jace's. So many amazing moments I've gotten to experience. But even still, there isn't enough money in the world to get me to go back and relive my tweens and teens.

All the self-doubt.

The wanting to fit in.

The fear of standing out.

And I had an entire army of family surrounding me.

A whole crew of cousins and siblings I knew were by my side through all of it.

I try to decide what I want to say to this little girl, who means everything to the man inside that house. The one who's slowly starting to mean everything to me.

No pressure . . .

"You know . . ." I lean forward so I can see a little further down the lake. "I have a ton of family. Like more family than any one person should ever have."

She doesn't look at me. Her shoulders stay tight as she presses her palms harder into the dock, probably wishing it would swallow her whole, or that I'd stop talking.

But I refuse to give up yet.

There's no turning back now.

"My mom is one of about a million brothers and sisters." I laugh, hoping to break the ice, but that's a fail. "Well, not really a million. But she is one of nine."

That doesn't seem to impress Kennedy, so I keep going, probably digging myself a bigger hole. "When you have that much family around you all the time, it can be a little . . . Let's call it overwhelming. You're never alone, even though, at times, you wish you could be. Everyone is always in your business, and the family gossip train is intense. But it had its good points too. Even if my mom was traveling for work with the team, or my dad was out of town with one of his fighters, there was always someone there for me. Someone besides my parents who I could trust to take care of me and my brother and sister. I always knew I was safe and loved. I always knew there would be someone there to listen and help."

She pulls her knees up to her chest and wraps her arms around them, closing herself off completely before slowly turning her head my way. "Are you and my dad gonna have more kids?"

"Oh, Kennedy . . ." I resist the urge to wrap her in a big hug. This kid would not appreciate that. "Your dad and I aren't anywhere near ready to even think about that. The only thing we're focused on right now is making sure you're comfortable in this house. And once you are, maybe you and I can work on being friends." I hold my breath, hoping that was the right answer.

"Does the puppy have a name?" she whispers.

I run a hand over Winnie's back and offer up a silent thank-you for the way she just nudged Kennedy to drop her legs so she could lounge in her lap. "Her name is Winston Churchill. But I call her Winnie."

"Does Winnie live here?" This time her question is a little less hesitant.

I nod my head gently. "She will. Your dad and I are still working everything out. But I'll be living here very soon, and Winnie will be coming with me when I do."

The puppy's snores grow louder as she nuzzles her little head against Kennedy's belly, and the little girl smiles softly for the first time since she walked through the door. "My dad travels a lot for work," she murmurs.

"He does." I nod as I carefully consider my next words. "Maybe you and I can come up with our own special routine when he's out of town. Kind of a girls' night thing."

She doesn't answer but doesn't look away either, so I'll take it as a bit more progress.

"Could Winnie sleep with me?" she whispers, and I couldn't hide my smile if you told me my life depended on it.

"I bet she'd like that. In case you can't tell, she's a snuggler."

"Mom never let me have a dog," she says as much to herself as to me.

"Well, your dad doesn't have a choice. Where I go, Winnie

goes. We're a package deal. She even comes to work with me."

Kennedy's little face lights up for a split-second before she hides her excitement. "That's cool."

Footsteps that aren't Deacon's fall behind us, and I catch Isla approaching from the corner of my eye.

"You two look deep in thought out here," she tells us.

Kennedy glances up at her mom and shrugs her shoulders, still quiet.

I'm good at a lot of things. Silence isn't one of them.

"I was just telling Kennedy how big my family is. One of my uncles actually lives next door. He's going to be one of your dad's assistant coaches. He has four kids, and the twins are Kennedy's age." A lightbulb goes off in my mind. "My cousin, Raven, lives on the other side of the lake, and she's your age too. We'll have to introduce you to them when you're ready."

I ignore the fact that my family doesn't know anything at all about Deacon and push down my own rapidly growing anxiety to try to focus on the little girl sitting next to me and how I can help her.

There will be plenty of time to freak out about telling my family I'm married after tonight.

Isla clasps her hands in front of her, seemingly excited. "That sounds perfect, doesn't it Kennedy? You'll be able to have friends before you start your new school."

Kennedy doesn't look at either of us before she gets up, brushes off her shorts, and waits patiently to see if Winnie is going to follow her. Maybe sensing Kennedy needs it, Winnie takes her lead and trots after her back to the house.

Isla looks at me, letting her smile fall and her eyes, so similar to Kennedy's, pool with unshed tears. "Please don't judge her. She's such a good kid with such a big heart. Please promise me you'll try to learn to love her."

My heart cracks and splinters into a million tiny pieces as I take Isla's hand in mine. "She's a kid facing a ton of big changes all at once. I can't even begin to act like I know what that feels like for a nine-year-old. She's allowed to process that any way she needs to without ever being judged by me. I just want to be here for her."

Isla throws her arms around me and cries, "I'm not sure how I'm supposed to live so far away from my baby. Please take care of her. Her and Deacon. I may not love him the way you do, but he's Kennedy's dad, and I'll always love him for giving me her. He deserves to be happy."

In that moment, it becomes easy to look past Isla's extroverted facade and see her for what she is right now. A heartbroken mother, trying to do what's best for her daughter, even if it's not what's best for her. And as I hug her back, I wonder if that's what my own mother has been going through.

Maybe Kennedy coming into my life was meant to be.

Maybe I need this little girl as much as she needs me.

DEACON

"Call if you need me, okay?" Isla pulls Kennedy in for a hug, like she's leaving for Japan now instead of in a week.

"I'm fine, Mom," my kid answers in that way kids do when they're completely over a situation. The plan had been for her to spend the night with me tonight to give her a bit of a feel for the house before she officially moves in next week. Baby steps typically work well for her. But somewhere along the way tonight, Isla got it in her head that it may be too much for Kennedy.

I'm not really sure if it is or not, but my daughter has officially fallen madly in love with Brynlee's dog, and that may actually be the only reason she wants to stay.

Potato. *Po-tah-to.*

I don't give a shit why she's comfortable enough to stay. I'm just glad she's not shutting down. If Winnie's the reason, I'll treat her better than any dog has ever been treated before. Score one for Brynlee because I've got a pretty good feeling that her getting Winnie may have had something to do with Kennedy, even if she's not admitting it.

This tiny little fearless woman hasn't stopped surprising me since the day she came back into my life and choked on a damn cherry. And now she's my wife. Nothing about this summer is going how I was expecting it to go. But it's surpassed every expectation I've had. If all goes well with Kennedy moving in, I may just be the luckiest son of a bitch to ever live.

Isla hugs our daughter one more time, then follows Shaun through the door before Kennedy turns to me. "Can Winnie sleep in my bed tonight?"

Brynlee wraps an arm around my waist, and I can feel the smile that's growing on her face. If these two ever decide to work together, I'm fucking doomed.

"Winnie's Brynlee's dog. You'll have to ask her," I let Kennedy know. And my wife inconspicuously slides her hand down and pinches my ass.

Kennedy takes a minute, then looks at Brynlee, who's currently tucked into my side.

Where she damn well belongs.

"Would it be okay if Winnie sleeps with me, Brynlee?" Her words are soft, but her eye contact is great, and that's something my girl struggles with. Baby steps. I'll take that as a win.

"Sure," Brynn beams. "I happen to have a brand-new dog bed in my car. I just hadn't brought it in earlier. Should we put that in your room?"

Kennedy nods with excitement sparkling in her eyes.

"How about you go get a shower, and I'll grab Winnie's stuff from Brynn's car." I wait until she's at the top of the stairs. "Everything is in the closet in your bathroom."

"Thanks, Dad." She disappears down the hall, and I spin Brynlee in my arms. "I think that went pretty well. Don't you?"

Fuck . . . I hadn't realized how relieved I am.

Was it perfect? Hell no.

But did everything go smoother than I expected? Thankfully, it did.

Brynn presses her hands against my chest as her soft scent wraps around me. "I think it went very well. And I think Winnie was our little superstar. Kennedy and she are going to be inseparable, just you watch."

I pull her in against me and rest my chin on her head. "You're a damn rockstar, you know that, wife?"

"You think?" She laughs and drags her hands down to the front of my jeans. "Because I can think of a few ways you could show me just how much you appreciated that rockstar status."

This woman . . . She's fucking perfect. "Oh, I already have plans for you tonight. And they start with you coming on my cock after you've come on my tongue."

Her body trembles against mine, and my cock presses against her ass, anticipating everything that's still in store.

"Deacon . . . Kennedy is here, and she's going to be sleeping across the hall."

"Yeah, baby. She is." I bend my head down next to her ear. "And her room doesn't have access to that balcony. Do you think you can be quiet for me?"

She shakes her head slowly, then brings my hand up to her lips and kisses my fingers. "If I get too loud . . . you may have to find something to shove in my mouth, husband. Do you think you could come up with something?"

Fuck me. She's going to kill me. But I'll die a happy man.

Finally getting to read a chapter of Harry Potter with my daughter in my house is something I've looked forward to since negotiations with the Revolution started. Having her in her own room under my roof is a small luxury I hope to never take for granted because man, it feels good.

I kiss her forehead and pull her pale purple comforter up around her, then close our new copy of *The Goblet of Fire* and place it on her nightstand. "No reading ahead without me. Okay?"

"I won't," she promises, then looks down at Winnie on the floor. "Why can't she sleep in my bed?"

"Because she's small. If she falls off your bed, she could get hurt. She's safer on her dog bed." I walk across the room and rest my hand over the light switch. "Do you want them on or off?"

"Off. But Dad . . . ?"

I stand, waiting for her question, wondering if she's going to keep fighting this fight.

"Do you think Brynlee likes me?"

Shit. I might as well have taken a stick to the face for as hard as that just hit. I stay where I am, conscious of not crowding her since she waited for me to be on the other side of the room before asking. "I know she likes you, kiddo. She liked you before she met you."

"But she didn't know me then. How could she like me?" she pushes back.

"It might be hard to believe, but she knew you before she met you because I never stop talking about you. Brynlee is the kind of person who pays attention to everything. She wants to know everyone, and she wants all the people in her life to know how much she cares. I'm not completely convinced she didn't get Winnie as much for you as she did for herself."

Kennedy's face beams. "I think I like her too. You smile when you look at her."

Out of the mouths of babes.

"Yeah, kiddo. I guess I do."

"Why didn't you have a big wedding?" she questions, and I wish she'd asked this earlier when Brynn was around to help me out.

"I'm not really sure, to be honest. We knew what we wanted, and we didn't want to wait." When all else fails, go with the truth. I wait to see if she asks anything else before shutting off the light. "Love you, kiddo."

"Love you, too, Dad."

Brynlee

There's a comfy lounge chair on Deacon's balcony that I make myself at home in as storm clouds roll in across the lake. I've got my iPad in my hand and my new book pulled up, but considering I've read the same chapter at least five times and haven't retained a word of it, I decide to give up for the night and just enjoy the view.

The covered roof gives enough protection that even when the storm from this morning starts back up again, I'm not getting wet. Everything about it is cozy and peaceful. And there goes that word again.

I haven't felt much peace since I found out my biological mother was gone.

Not since the day my biological grandparents, who I've never spoken to, called my father and told him my mother had died.

I remember thinking I should be sad.

But I wasn't.

I was too busy being scared of what it meant.

"What are you thinking about?" Deacon interrupts my spiraling thoughts. His hands hang above his head from the doorframe, and he leans outside.

This man is beautiful, inside and out, and for right now, he's mine.

"I was thinking about peace, and how I hadn't felt much of it there for a little while," I admit, thinking how sad that sounds.

He drops his arms and closes the distance between us. "What changed?"

I slide my palms into his and stand up. "I guess the answer is you. You quieted my fears. You keep saying how much I'm helping you. But I swear to you, Deacon, you're giving me more than you know."

He opens his mouth to speak, but I cover it with my finger. "Just let me get this out," I whisper as the rain picks up around us, silencing the rest of the world. I try to find the words that won't come. The words I so desperately need to tell him, but even the idea of them petrify me in a way nothing ever has. "I'm falling in love with you, and there's so much you don't even know."

He wraps a big hand around my head and bends his knees until we're at eye level. "You'll tell me when you're ready, baby."

He presses his lips to mine and licks into my mouth, and I melt in his arms.

Here, I'm safe.

Nothing can hurt me, and no test can define me. With Deacon, it feels safe. I feel safe.

He tastes like bourbon and chocolate, and I can't get enough as I press up onto my toes and wrap myself around my husband. My lips skim up his neck as his hands gather the hem of my sundress and slide it up over my ass before he runs a finger over my silk panties.

Deacon spins me around and presses me forward against the bronze balcony railing. "Ass in the air, red."

He drops to his knees behind me and presses his face against my pussy. "So fucking wet for me already. Fuck, Brynn . . ." The words are a guttural growl against my sensitive skin as his hot breath goes right through the satin covering my drenched sex.

I peek over my shoulder and whimper at the sinful sight behind me.

"You gotta be quiet, baby. If you moan . . . if you make a single sound, this stops." He kisses the inside of my thigh, and I bite down on my lips. "Just like that, baby. Be a good girl for me, and let me taste your cunt, wife."

I turn my head back as my pussy throbs from his delicious words.

Every time this man calls me *wife*, I get hotter. Wetter. Guess I found my kink.

Heat rolls off his skin as he peels my panties down my legs and smooths a hand over my bare ass before he smacks it, sending a hot pulse straight to my throbbing core.

"Deacon," I whisper, praying the heavy rain drowns out any sound.

"You like that, don't you?" His rough palm rubs over the undoubtedly bright red handprint he left on my pale skin. When I squirm back against him, he presses a warm, wet kiss against my skin. "Fuck, Brynn . . ."

"Deacon . . ." I silently scream when that same hand slaps my pussy before he finally presses his lips to my clit and sucks.

I push back against him and drop my head down to the railing, desperate for more. And Deacon doesn't hold back as he eats me, bringing me to orgasm over and over again. Refusing to stop his delicious assault. And my God, he works his fingers, his lips . . . his whole fucking hand while he eats me until he's rung every last drop from me, and I'm silently screaming as I come with the most explosive orgasm.

And just as I sag against the railing, cool air hits my overheated skin and a whimper builds in my throat until Deacon pulls my dress over my head and stands behind me, gloriously naked.

He wraps my hair around his fist and pulls my head back until his lips are grazing my ear.

"Tell me I don't have to be gentle tonight, Brynn. I'm not sure I can be." Deacon's deep voice promises so much more than I could ever ask for.

I lean forward and turn my head, barely able to stand up on my shaking legs. "Don't be gentle, Deacon. You won't hurt me. I won't break." I push back against him, and Deacon drags his cock through my sex, teasing me.

"You are fucking perfect, wife." He thrust into me in one powerful stroke, seating himself deeper than he's ever been before, stealing my last breath from my lungs.

He doesn't give my aching pussy time to adjust to his size.

One strong hand grips my face, holding my mouth to his, swallowing every moan and whimper as our tongues duel for control while his fingers work my clit as he fucks me in a beautiful, brutal rhythm.

I claw at his skin with every delicious snap of his hips.

My body feels like an exposed nerve. Raw and hypersensitive. Overwhelmed.

The way his dick drags against my walls, hitting that spot inside me I never truly believed existed, over and over . . . I just can't . . . can't think . . . can't breathe . . . can't focus on anything but the way I feel right now as he fucks me harder. *Faster*. Then just when I feel my orgasm barreling down again, he growls against my face, "Don't even think about coming yet, Brynn. We're not done yet."

"Deacon, oh God . . . I can't . . . *Please*," I plead.

"Not yet, baby." His lips are everywhere, greedy for the taste of my skin as pleasure wars with pain, bringing me to new heights I never knew existed.

Rough fingers dig into both hips in a bruising hold, and I'm pulled down onto his hard cock. And when I'm sure I can't take any more, his hand slips between my legs, running through my soaked sex, and drags my juices along the crack of my ass, circling without pushing inside.

"Oh, God. Deacon. I can't . . ." I plead as my legs threaten to give out, and without warning, he plunges one finger inside me, stealing my last shred of sanity.

It burns and stings and somehow feels so fucking good as he slams into my pussy over and over while he fucks my virgin ass. First with one finger, then two, until I shatter in a pulsing, throbbing orgasm, unable to see anything but a kaleidoscope of colors in front of my eyes.

Deacon seals his lips over mine, swallowing my hoarse screams while I shake under him until he explodes inside me, filling me completely.

"My fucking wife," he whispers against my mouth as he fucks me through another orgasm, any semblance of control from either of us completely eviscerated.

The world around us ceases to exist as I'm lifted in strong arms and carried to the bed.

Deacon pulls me against him, and I drift off, knowing nothing will ever be the same.

The Philly Press

KROYDON KRONICLES

JUST THE TIP...

Have you ever heard a rumor so juicy you can't wait to sink your teeth into it?
Well, this reporter has been given a tip that I'm still working to confirm.
Until then, let me wet your palate with this:
another Kroydon Hills hottie may be off the market.
Details coming soon!

#KroydonKronicles

DEACON

༄

I wake up the next morning, expecting to find Brynlee next to me. But when I reach for her, the bed is empty—again. One of these goddamn days, this woman is going to still be in bed in the morning. After a quick shower —that's more than necessary since I smell like sex . . . *really fucking good sex* . . . and I have a nine-year-old, who's also somewhere in this house—I go on a hunt for the ladies in my life.

They're easy enough to find. I just have to follow the sound of giggling and the smell of coffee and bacon. Brynlee's plating up scrambled eggs and bacon, while Kennedy sits on the floor with Winnie between her legs, playing tug of war with a squeaky, purple polka-dotted dinosaur.

"Morning girls." I walk up behind Brynn and press a kiss to her head.

"Good morning, Coach." She runs her thumb over my lips and smiles a sweet kind of smile, and I'm reminded of what she said last night about peace. "There's bacon and eggs on the counter, and coffee is in the pot. Kit Kat, make sure you wash your hands before you eat."

THE SWEET SPOT

Kennedy pops right up and goes over to the sink. "Okay, Brynnie. Do you want orange juice, Dad?"

I clear my throat and look between the two of them and wonder what kind of alternate universe I woke up in. "Kit Kat?"

Brynn and Kennedy give each other some kind of an inside look, and swear to God, I may pinpoint that as the moment I fell in love with my wife. Although it's probably more like the moment I realized it. Pretty sure I fell weeks ago.

"So," Brynn starts. "Your daughter asked what she should call me."

"Yeah, Dad." Kennedy hops up on a counter stool with the ketchup in her hand and adds some eggs to her plate. "I heard you call her Brynn and Brynlee last night. So I asked what I should call her."

"Then we talked about nicknames and how my friends and family like to call me Brynnie," Brynn fills in, as if they're finishing each other's thoughts. What the fuck? How long was I sleeping?

"So I decided I wanted to call her Brynnie. And she asked if I had a nickname."

Brynn hands Kennedy a glass of orange juice and me a cup of coffee. "My friends are really big on nicknames, so Kennedy and I came up with Kit Kat. I mean, you named her Kennedy Kane, so Kit Kat seems perfect."

Kennedy nods her head, like this all makes perfect sense, and I'm left wondering what the hell changed while I was sleeping. But my kid and my wife are both smiling . . . hell, even the dog is smiling, so I'm going to keep my mouth shut and be grateful. I drop a kiss on Kennedy's head and grab a plate.

"All right, then. I guess that makes sense." I look over at

Brynlee when Kennedy's not paying attention and silently mouth, *Thank you.*

She steals a piece of bacon from my plate, then rests her hip on the counter next to me. "Listen, I need to go check on Gracie. She and Ares are going through a thing, and I've been kind of rough on her."

"Why have you been rough?" I ask, knowing it's not like Brynn to be rough on anyone.

"Because I'm worried about her. She refuses to put her long-term health first, and every now and then, everyone needs a little tough love."

I lift a brow and whisper. "Tough love, huh?"

Her blush is instant, but so is her smile. "You're incorrigible."

"Yeah . . . but you love it," I tease.

"Maybe I do," she agrees with an incredibly sexy gleam in her green eyes before she grabs Winnie's leash. "I'm going to take her for a walk."

I watch her go, then focus on Kennedy. "So Kit Kat, huh?"

She nods.

"Like the candy?" I ask, and she nods again.

She's going to love this nickname, and some guy is gonna want to eat her *candy* one day, and I'm going to have to kill him. I can see it already.

"Listen, kid. I've got an idea. If Brynlee has to leave soon, how about you and I run to a store before I bring you back to your mom's? I could use your help picking out a gift. Sound good to you?"

"Is the gift for Brynnie?" Kennedy asks, intrigued.

"Yes, it is. And I'm going to need it to be a surprise, so you can't tell her. Okay?"

"Okay." She hops off the stool and puts her plate in the sink. "I'm going to go get dressed." She darts upstairs, and a plan starts to come together.

*B*rynn leaves soon after, and Kennedy and I wait to run our errand until after she's gone. By the time I drop her off at her mom's that afternoon, we've had a really great day together.

It's been one of the best days I can remember having in a long damn time.

The kind of day that makes you feel good about life.

I'm driving through town when my phone rings with an incoming call from Brynn.

"Hey, red. What's up?"

"Deacon . . ." she sobs.

"Brynlee—where are you? Are you okay? What's wrong, baby?" My heart races as I turn the car around, desperate to get to her.

"I'm okay." Her breath catches in her throat. "I'm at my condo." Another sob. "Can you come here, please?"

"I'll be right there, baby. Don't hang up. Tell me what's wrong."

She sobs again, and I can't understand what she's saying, so I press the damn gas pedal to the floor to get to her as fast as I can. "You're scaring me, Brynn. Talk to me. I'm almost there."

"It's Ares . . ." She hiccups, and my rage suddenly has a target.

"I'll fucking kill him if he hurt you."

"No . . ." she cries harder. "Just come here, please. I need you."

She ends the call, and I hold my breath until I get to her

building and race up to her place. "Brynn..." I pound on her door. "Open the door, Brynlee."

A door down the hall opens, and a woman looks out at me just before Brynn answers.

And holy shit, when she does, I'm not prepared for the complete devastation on her beautiful face.

"Baby." I step inside and cup her face in my hands, forcing her to look at me. "What happened?"

She pulls back, broken and sobbing, her arms wrapped around herself, barely holding it together.

"Brynn, you've got to tell me something. Help me here. I don't know what happened. I don't—" My words die on my tongue when she shakes her head and looks away, leaving me helpless and guessing.

"Cross and Ares's dad . . ." Her breath catches, and another tear falls. "He's dead. He just died. Ares was just there last week, and he was fine, and now he's dead." Her tears fall faster as her shoulders shake with each new sob. "Grace and Nix flew up to Maine to be with them."

Her knees give out, and I catch her before she falls and carry her to the couch.

I sit down with her on my lap and hold my wife as she breaks in front of my eyes.

"Were you close with him?" I ask, not having any idea how to help. She's talked about Cross and Ares and the Sinclair twins before, but never about the Wilders' dad.

She shakes her head no and cries harder. "I only met him once. It's just . . . life is so short. And we really don't have any control over *how* it ends or *when* it ends." Her breaths come out short. Panicked.

Fuck. I know what's coming next.

Her face pales. "I can't breathe—"

"You're having a panic attack, baby," I tell her calmly and wrap my arms around her, then press her against me in a deep pressure hold. The added weight has helped Kennedy before.

"Breathe with me, Brynn. Can you match your breaths to mine, baby? In for three." I do it with her. "Hold for two." We wait two beats. "Then exhale."

We repeat this over a few times until eventually, she calms down enough to focus on my face, and the new tears that spring free morph into a different kind of pain. "I don't want to die, Deacon."

I press my lips to her forehead and hold them there. "You're not dying for a long time. You're going to live a long, happy life. And I'm going to be right there, making sure you're smiling every day."

"You don't understand . . . " she tells me through quivering lips. "My biological grandparents reached out to my dad at the beginning of the summer. We don't have any relationship with them. Never have. So it was weird when he told us they called. Then his face . . ." She closes her eyes as if reliving a memory. "I'll never forget that face as long as I live. They'd called to tell him my biological mom had died." The sob that rips from her body barely sounds human.

"I'm so sorry, Brynn. I can't even imagine how hard that was to hear." I hold her so damn close, wishing I could take this pain away from her.

"That's the thing. At first, I felt awful because I didn't feel anything. I didn't know her. She was never a part of my life. She literally dumped me on my dad as a baby and never looked back unless it was for money. I wasn't heartbroken when I heard." She closes her eyes, and a thick tear catches in her lashes. "I was numb."

When she finally opens them, her tear-filled green eyes focus on me for the first time since I walked in, and I see my girl behind the devastation.

"I swear I've tried to tell you this so many times already,

Deacon. But every time I've tried, I froze. Once I say it, I can't un-say the words, and I've spent months not saying the words."

"I'm not following you, Brynn..."

Fear is a funny thing. You think you know fear the first time you're in a car accident. Or the first time you break a bone.

Then you have a kid, and fear takes on a whole new meaning. The way you fear you won't be enough to keep them safe.

But the fear I feel now is entirely different. It's the kind of fear you can't possibly comprehend until the woman you love is talking about dying. Unable to breathe. Unable to calm down.

The kind of fear that precedes the worst kind of news.

The kind that changes everything.

"Brynlee..." No other words come as I hold onto her like she's my lifeline.

She holds my cheek in her hand and closes her eyes. "My mom died of Huntington's disease, Deacon."

"What?" I ask, sure I just heard her wrong as my brain drags up everything I've ever heard about Huntington's. And none of it's good. "*What?*"

"Huntington's disease. It's a death sentence. There's no cure. A person diagnosed today can live as little as ten years from their diagnosis." Big, fat tears stream down her face. "And it's genetic. If your parent has it, there's a fifty/fifty chance you'll inherit it from them."

The axe falls hard and swift.

I just found her.

I've barely gotten to love her.

I can't lose her.

"Brynlee... No. We'll hire the best doctors in the world. I haven't spent a penny of my money. I've saved it all. We'll go wherever we have to. They're always doing experimental things in Switzerland. We'll go there. We don't have to accept this. There's got to be something we can do."

Her lips tremble as her thumb runs over my cheek, catching the tear I hadn't realized had fallen. "I wanted to tell you so many times—"

"Why didn't you? Did you think I wouldn't be here? Did you think I would run?" I ask, so fucking hurt.

"Deacon . . . we didn't get married because we were madly in love." She shakes her head, like that makes any difference.

"I just found you. I'm not going to lose you," I tell her, absolutely refusing to accept there's nothing we can do. "There's always something that can be done. We just have to find it."

"I don't know if I carry the gene, Deacon. I haven't been tested yet. I'm scared. I'm not sure I want to know. If it's positive, will I live every day, wondering if this is the day the symptoms start? Will I always wonder if today's the day my countdown starts? I could live another twenty years before the first symptom hits, but if I carry the gene, I won't have kids. I can't. Not if I'd be doing this to them too. I've researched it, Deacon. It's not an easy life, and it's an awful death."

"Jesus, Brynn. Is it better to live life not knowing? Not being able to do everything we can to prevent or slow the disease down before you get any symptoms? Isn't it better to be prepared than to live not knowing whether you carry the damn gene?" The words come out harsh, but I'm so fucking angry right now. At her. At the world.

"You said there's a fifty/fifty chance. What if you don't have it? What if you're fine and you spend your life wondering *what if* when you could have spent your life living?"

"I'm so scared, Deacon . . ." she whispers as her chest shakes with every shattered breath.

"Let me be your strength, Brynn. I'll give you mine when you don't have any left. We can get through this. But you've got to let me in." I tuck her against my chest and listen to her cries.

"What if it comes back positive . . . What then?" she asks weakly.

"What if it comes back negative . . ." I counter. "What then?"

"Brynlee," a man's voice hollers through the other side of her door, followed by a bang before the door slams open against the wall. "Brynlee—" The guy barges in, calling out for her but then focusing on me. "Who the fuck are you?" This asshole asks, not reading the situation at all, and it looks like I have a target for all this anger.

I put her on the couch behind me and get between her and him. "I'm her fucking husband. Who the fuck are you?"

"Her *what?*" The guy yells back, taking a step toward us with his fists balled at his sides.

He's a few inches shorter than me, but he's built like a fighter.

"What the fuck, Killian?" Brynn stands up and moves in front of me, trying to wipe her face.

"Killian?" I ask, looking from her to him, unsure what she's saying because my brain is still stuck on the fact that my wife could be dying.

"Yes," she pushes me back. "Killian. My brother." She looks behind the door that just put a hole in her wall. "Also the man who's going to fix that wall tomorrow."

"Brynnie, what the hell? Caitlin called and said some guy was screaming from the other side of your door. What the hell is going on in here? Did he hurt you?" he asks her, then turns his pissed-off glare on me. "What did you do to my sister?"

I move her behind me *again*.

MMA fighter or not, I will fucking kill him if he hurts her.

"Oh my God. Put your dicks away, both of you. He didn't hurt me, you bonehead," she yells at him, then turns to me. "And you. I guess we're going public now?"

"That's what you're worried about . . . right now?" I ask. "With everything going on, you still care about that?"

"Did you say *her husband?*" Killian asks, and Brynlee groans.

"Killer, if you say a single word to Mom and Dad, I swear to God, I'll screw with your equipment when you least expect it." And the way she says that sounds more than a little fucked up.

"What the hell is going on here?" he asks, and I turn to look at Brynn.

Her red eyes are swollen, puffy, and utterly exhausted. Tear streaks stain her cheeks, and I realize she's suddenly more worried about her parents finding out about us than she is about dying.

"You know what . . ." I tell her more calmly than I thought I was capable of. "When you figure that out, how about you come talk to me? Because a second ago, I was scared the woman I love was going to be taken from me. But apparently, you're more worried about your parents finding out you're married than you are about the fact that you let me and Kennedy both fall in love with you when you knew there was a chance you could be taken from us."

Oh yeah. The anger has kicked the fear's ass, because anger . . . anger I know.

Anger I can deal with. I can harness it.

Losing my wife . . . That I can't handle right now.

"How about you let me know when you figure out what really matters?" I kiss the top of her head and walk through the door, yanking it shut behind me.

BRYNLEE

**Sit with people who protect your name in rooms you aren't in.
Those are the women we want in our sandbox.**

—*Brynlee's Secret Thoughts*

"What the hell is wrong with you?" I cry out to my brother as I watch Deacon leave.

"What's wrong with *me*? What the hell is wrong with *you*, Brynnie? Did you marry the new hockey coach? And is he just now finding out about the Huntington's thing? And did you take the damn test yet?" Killian shouts right back in my face, the way only a brother can and would. And the worst part is everything he's saying is valid.

How is this my life?

When did I go from being a force of nature to a broken woman swaying in the wind?

"You know what?" I step closer to Killian and shove his chest. "Yes . . . Yes, I married the hockey coach. He has a name, and it's Deacon Kane. You might want to remember it, since he didn't back down from the big, scary fighter, now did he?"

I shove him again because indignation feels so much better than guilt and shame and fear. "He also has a beautiful daughter who I love. So not only am I married, but I'm a stepmom too. And I'm going to need you to keep your mouth shut until I tell Mom and Dad. Which will be soon."

"Brynnie . . ." Killian grabs my hands before I can hit him again.

"I will. I promise I will. But first I have to apologize to my husband, *the hockey coach*, because you know what? He said he loves me." Not sure if Deacon even realizes he said it, but even in my broken mind, I heard. And I'm choosing to cling to that in the mountain of a mess my life currently is. "And he's right. I let him fall in love with me—fuck, I let him marry me without being honest."

"What did you lie about, Brynn?" Killian asks in a way that reminds me that at least one person still thinks I'm a good person.

"I should told him I have an expiration date already ticking down. I should have told him about the Huntington's thing. But I didn't. You and Kenzie and Mom and Dad were the only ones who knew. I fucked up, Kill, and I need to fix it. I owe him that."

"Is he good to you, Brynn? Do you love him?" Kill's words stop me in my tracks.

"He's everything," I whisper.

"Nah, B. He's not. *You're* everything. But if he makes you happy, go tell him. If he's smart, he'll forgive you." Killian pulls me in for a hug and lifts me from my feet. "You think I can be there when you tell Mom and Dad? I want to see the look on Mom's face." His evil smile is the same today as it was when he was ten years old and tried to get a picture of Everly Sinclair changing into her bikini in our pool house.

"I may need you there to hold Dad back. I think he's going to react worse than Mom." I wipe my face and square my shoulders. "So, if you'll excuse me, I have to go find Deacon and beg him to forgive me."

Killian sidesteps me, stopping me from passing by. "Does that mean you you're going to take the test?"

I stop and look at my little brother, and my heart breaks all over again. "I'm scared, Killian. I'm scared I'm going to take the test and it'll come back positive. If I don't know, I can act like it doesn't matter." My heart shatters into a million tiny pieces as I put words to my greatest fear.

He drags his thumb over my cheek, wiping away my tears. "But it does matter. You matter, and you're putting yourself and everyone who loves you through hell, Brynn."

"I'm sorry I'm hurting you, Kill. But I owe the man who just walked through that door an explanation and a conversation before I can make any decision."

He steps back with a nod. "Love you, Brynn."

"Love you too, Kill. Make sure you fix my door before you go. And do you think you can take Winnie for the night? She's hiding somewhere. I think we were too loud for her."

"Yeah, I got her. You just go."

"Thanks, little brother." I grab my keys and purse and don't bother looking in a mirror before I leave. I've wasted enough time not being completely honest with my husband, and it's time I fixed that. I don't need to go far to find him because as soon as I open my door, Deacon is sitting on the floor in my hallway.

"What are you doing here?" My nerves kick into overdrive as I slide down the wall next to him and kick my legs out in front of myself, mirroring him, though his legs just go a lot farther out than mine do.

"I'm not really angry, it's easier to be mad than to admit I'm scared, so I left. But the second I was through the door, I was too damn far from you, Brynn. I figured I'd wait until your brother left so we could finish our conversation." He looks tired, and I hate knowing I did that to him. "Did everything go okay with Killian?"

I run my teeth over my lips, stalling. "It went. He's not thrilled with me, but he'll get over it."

"How are you feeling?" Deacon asks as he wraps his arm around my shoulder and pulls me against his side.

"You're still here, so I'm better than I thought I was." My heart cracks a little as I look at him. "I'm sorry I didn't tell you sooner. Telling you would have made it real, and I wasn't ready to accept it could be real."

"We deal with whatever the universe throws our way, Brynn. But I can't help you if I don't know. You can't keep things from me." He's being more understanding than I deserve. But this man sees me in a way no one else ever has, so why should I be surprised? "I can't force you to get the test, but I can hold your hand while you do it."

"If it comes back positive, we can't have kids, Deacon. That might not feel like a big deal now, but it might be in a few years," I tell him, blinking back more tears.

"We already have a kid. I guess if you count Winnie, we've got two. And if it's positive, we can adopt a whole hockey team if we want to. But I'm not worried about that. I'm worried about *you*. I want to give you the best life possible, and I want it to be the longest life possible. It might help if we know what we're up against."

"I don't deserve you," I press a gentle kiss to his lips. "Did you mean what you said in there?" I ask, needing to know the truth but then deciding I want him to hear it from me first.

"Because I'm in love with you, Deacon. I know what I said last night, but I'm not falling. I've already fallen. I fell weeks ago. Looking back, I think I was in love with you before you ever even came back from Boston."

He wraps a hand around my face and drags my forehead to his. "I'm so fucking in love with you, Brynlee St. James."

"Oh, thank God," I laugh lightly.

"I love your laugh and your smile and the way you drag your teeth over your bottom lip." He runs his thumb over my lips and sends chills dancing over my skin." I love the way you are with my kid. I love the way the world feels when you're next to me. And I'll love you through whatever else the world throws our way. Marry me."

My smile is instant as I let his words wash over me, forever grateful for this man. "I already married you," I whisper, and Deacon leans back slightly and pulls a teal ring box out of his pocket.

"Yeah. But you asked me last time. I needed to ask you this time." He cracks open the box, and a beautiful, brilliant-cut diamond solitaire and matching eternity band sparkle against the white velvet lining.

"They're beautiful, Deacon."

He pulls both rings out and slides them on my finger, and there go those butterflies in my stomach again.

"You know, you didn't have to get me rings to get me to tell my parents. I told Killian before I came out here I was going to talk to them. I just needed to make sure things were right with you first." My stomach flips over how my parents will take this news, but Deacon deserves so much more than to be hidden.

"Baby, you're already my wife, and that's all that matters. But I want to do it right this time. I want you in a white dress, walking down an aisle, and I want Kennedy there to watch us. I want you to take my name, and I want to wake up with you *in* my bed every day. And if that starts with us talking to your parents, then let's go talk to your parents." His lips tilt down. "But I think it needs to start with you taking control of your future. We need to be able to make plans, Brynn. One way or the other."

I've spent my summer trying to act like this test didn't exist.

As if it wasn't a big bad looming over my life.

I've given the test itself all the power, and as scary as it's going to be, it's time I take that power back.

"Will you come with me to take the test?' I ask him, petrified of his answer.

"There's nothing that would keep me away from you, red. We were always real."

I press my lips to his. "We were always real."

My door opens, and Killian stands there with Winnie in his hands. "Uh . . . does this mean I don't need to take your dog?"

"Any chance you feel like coming to Mom and Dad's with us?" I ask my brother while I squeeze my husband's hand.

"Like tonight?" Killian laughs like a little douche. "Dude, more like there's no way I'm missing this." The shit kicks Deacon's foot. "You might not know me, brother, but I might be the only reason you don't die tonight."

"Killian—" I shout as inappropriate laughter catches in my throat, the sweeping emotions of the day already taking their toll.

"What?" He looks at me with a smug smirk. "Too soon?"

"Yeah." I push up to my feet then and take Winnie from my brother. "Maybe just a little."

Deacon stands up and looks between me and Killian. "I guess we didn't actually meet." He offers him his hand. "Deacon."

Kill smiles. "Oh, I know who you are. I'm just wondering

who's gonna go for the throat first, Mom or Dad. Hope you've got good reflexes."

Deacon looks at me, and I smile. "He's not wrong."

"You sure you don't want to call them first, Brynn?" Deacon asks as we turn onto my parents' street, following behind Killian's Jeep. "Maybe give them some kind of a heads-up?"

I think about it again and visualize just how that conversation would go over the phone, and my imagination is probably worse than reality could ever be. "Honestly, no. I don't want to lose my nerve. Not just because I'm about to tell my parents I got married but because of everything else that's going on. This way is better, trust me."

I have no idea how this is going to go.

And when we pull into their circular driveway, and my brother jumps down from his massive Jeep and bounces on his toes, I decide maybe bringing him wasn't the best idea. "You're way to excited about this, Kill."

I let Winnie out of the car, and she runs to Killian.

The little traitor.

I walk over to Deacon, and he rests his palm on the small of my back. "Lead the way, Brynn."

I brush my lips over his before I move. "Just remember, you can't divorce me if my parents are assholes."

"One day, some cocksucker is going to want to marry Kennedy, and we're probably going to hate him. If he were to show up at our house and tell us they got married without even meeting us, we'd be pretty pissed. Try to remember that when your parents get mad, and everything will be fine." He presses me forward, and I stare at him in shock.

"Why are you so calm?" I ask, jealous of his ability to compartmentalize like that.

"Because you're worth it," he tells me. Then he leans down and whispers in my ear, "Now let's get this over with. I'm thinking makeup sex is going to be the perfect way to end the day."

"Umm . . . I think you may have broken me last night, husband," I tease.

"Then I'll just have to be gentle tonight, wife. Now quit stalling."

By the time we make it to the front door, it's open, and Killian is nowhere to be found.

Noted. Winnie and he are both traitors.

"Hello—" I call out as Deacon and I walk in the foyer of my parents' house, receiving no answer. I take his hand in mine, trying to absorb some of his calm. "We moved here when I was little. Right after Mom had Livvy."

I guide Deacon through the enormous house Mom always made sure felt like a home, not a museum. She wanted us to be kids at home. She didn't care if we got handprints on the walls or peanut butter on the counters. There were no prying cameras or reporters here. It was our sanctuary, and I try to keep that in mind now as I search for her and Dad.

Deacon pulls me to a stop in front of an old family portrait. "Look at you." He points. "Jesus, your family is big."

I smother a laugh. "Yeah, and this is a really old picture. We're twice this size now. I was maybe eight in this picture. It's before Kenzie and Easton joined the family. Before half my uncles were married. Before I had any idea what my life would become."

"That's the kind of innocence I want to make sure we give Kennedy for as long as we can," he muses.

My God. I love this man.

"We will." I kiss his cheek, and a throat clears behind us.

Fuck. I look past my giant of a husband. "Hi, Mom."

"Brynlee," she says very carefully. "And Coach Kane. I didn't expect to find you in my house today, kissing my daughter, no less."

"Scarlet." Deacon offers her his hand, and she looks at it like a bug on the floor she doesn't want to dirty her Manolos by squishing.

"Oh, we're not in the office today, Deacon. You can call me, Mrs. St. James."

Well . . . shit.

"Your father is outside by the pool, smoking cigars with Becket and Sam. Why don't you head out back." Her smile is evil, and my stomach drops as I watch her walk away.

"You sure you're ready for this?" I ask Deacon with a new level of nerves.

He tilts his head to look around me, unable to see where my mother went. "Becket. Your uncle, the senator?"

I nod my head. "And Sam . . . Beneventi."

"Another uncle?" he asks as he tries to place the name.

"Yeah, my cousin Maddox's dad. He's . . ."

"Is he the one I've seen on the news? The one they've tried to connect to the Mafia?" Deacon asks with a flash of something in his eyes.

"They've never proven that," I tell him. "But let's just say he's probably the most powerful man in Philadelphia." We don't ever discuss or confirm Uncle Sam's business. "They're Dad's best friends. The three of them went to high school together."

Deacon nods. "Doesn't change anything for me, Brynn. But if you don't want them here while we discuss any of it,"—

he means the Huntington's—"you just tell me, and I'll ask them to leave."

Yup. I love him.

I also want him to live to see tomorrow, so I'm not going to let him do that.

I lace my fingers in his and make my way through the house to face the firing squad.

It's time.

DEACON

As we walk outside, I'm immediately drawn to the table by the outdoor kitchen where Scarlet stands between three men, a bottle of bourbon between them that costs more than my first car. Cade St. James doesn't look much different than he did a decade ago. A little more gray in his hair, and a few more lines on his face don't change the fact that this man is an MMA champion, who, even past his prime, could still stand toe-to-toe with me, and I'm no fucking slouch.

I easily recognize the man next to him as Senator Becket Kingston, which means the third must be Sam Beneventi. Between these three, one is going to want to kill me, one probably wouldn't hesitate to pull the trigger, and the third could probably make it look like an accident.

I'm used to walking into tough rooms. A hockey locker room is full of fearless men. But they play with rules. The collective power between these three kings means there are no rules, and I'm about to steal the princess out of the tower.

"Daddy." Brynlee hesitates as we stop next to the table.

Jesus Christ, she just called him *Daddy*. I'm fucking screwed.

Cade looks from his wife to his daughter, completely ignoring me, and I notice Killian out of the corner of my eye, grabbing a beer from an outdoor refrigerator. The fucker smiles from ear to ear. Yeah. He's looking forward to this.

"Brynnie. I didn't expect to see you tonight." Cade lifts his glass and looks over at the way my hand is holding Brynn's and lifts his brow. "Didn't expect to see you either, Kane."

"Kane," Becket says. "The kid from Block Island?"

Scarlet leans her hip against her husband's chair and smiles condescendingly at her brother. "Do you even read the King Corp. emails, Becks? Deacon is the Revolution's new head coach." Her words may sound like she's not upset that I'm here with her daughter, but the look on her face says otherwise.

"Why's the coach holding Brynn's hand?" The third guy asks and puts his cigar down with an underlying anger in his words.

And I wait for it.

Because I know it's coming.

Tick. Tick. Boom.

"And why the fuck is there a diamond ring on her finger?" Sam points out as he leans back in his chair and crosses his arms over his chest.

"That's why we're here," Brynn tells them, then looks at her uncles. "We were hoping to talk to Mom and Dad alone." She squeezes my hand, and I'm not sure if she's trying to comfort me or herself.

I drop her hand and wrap an arm around her waist.

She doesn't need to comfort me. I can hold my own, and no one at this table is changing anything between us. When I go to bed tonight, it'll be with my wife.

"Not a chance, Brynn." Becket grins and sips his bourbon

as Killian pulls out a chair that his mother immediately pushes back in.

"What?" he asks, and Scarlet shakes her head and points at Brynn's uncles.

"They get to stay. You go inside."

He shakes his head and looks at his dad and uncles. "If it makes a difference, he was ready to come to blows with me earlier if I even looked at her wrong. And I'm a scary motherfucker."

"I'm scarier," Sam says quietly, and Cade glares at his son.

Killian turns back to Brynn. "I tried."

"Go," she whispers to him.

Brynlee waits until her brother is inside before pulling out her own chair across the table from her uncles and taking a seat. "You aren't surprised."

Well, damn . . . I wasn't expecting that.

"The fuck I'm not, Brynn." Becket laughs, but Scarlet and Cade just look at her. "You knew."

"The second Judge Guiliano got your call, she called me," her mother tells her before finishing what's left of Cade's bourbon and pouring another glass. "There's nothing that happens in this city that one of us doesn't know, Brynlee. No more questions from you. Now it's our turn."

I stand behind Brynn, watching the dynamic play out. This family is complicated as hell, but I won't hesitate to take her out of here if they upset her.

"Why did we have to find out from a friend you were even seeing someone, let alone getting married? Really, Brynn. What's gotten into you?" Scarlet nails her daughter with her words.

"I know what's gotten into her," Becket snickers, and I clench my fist.

"Out," Cade barks, and Sam grabs Becket's shirt.

"Dumb fuck," Sam groans. "I'm going to remind you that

you said that one day when it's Kenzie seeing someone. Let's go."

"And miss this?" Becket argues but stands up anyway, then points a finger at me. "Keep in mind I can erase any trace of your existence if you hurt my niece, Kane."

"Lay off the bourbon, Becks," his sister chastises as she watches the two men join Killian in the house.

"Are you happy?" Cade asks. "They're gone. Now start talking."

I'm already over this whole shit show. "I love your daughter. Do I wish I had come to you first and asked your permission to marry her?" I want to tell him *fuck no, I don't*, but he's Brynn's father, and I owe him more respect than that. "As a father of a little girl, I'd like to think I should have. But in reality, I don't need it. I need hers. She needs to know I'm a good man. She needs to believe I'll protect her with my dying breath. She's the only person who matters, and that's how it should be."

Brynn grabs my hand and squeezes again.

"Does he know?" her mother asks, seemingly dismissing everything I just said.

"He does," Brynn tells her with a shake in her voice, which kicks my protective instincts into overdrive. "He's taking me to get the test."

That's when Scarlet's perfect facade cracks. Her face falls, and a gasp gets stuck in her throat as she lays her hand on her husband's and looks at me with tears quickly filling her eyes. "And you'll be there, no matter what those results are?" she asks as her first tear falls.

"Yes," is the only word I manage before I blow out my own breath, trying to maintain some sense of control over the consequences she's concerned with.

"We just wanted to get married. Just us. But we were thinking about doing something small that would include

Deacon's daughter, Kennedy. Just us and our families," she tells them both, and Cade groans.

"That's not small, Brynn." He shakes his head.

"What if we did it at your parents' inn, Deacon?" Scarlet asks as she silently looks at me with something like approval in her eyes.

"Whatever Brynn wants," I answer with eyes only for my wife.

"Brynnie?" Scarlet asks, waiting not so patiently.

"Something small, Mom. And maybe wait until I get the results. I don't know that I'll want to do anything after that if they're not what I want to hear." The elephant in the room just trampled over my fucking heart with one fucking sentence.

"I'd like to do it before the season starts next month." I sit down next to Brynn and force her to look at me. To really listen to what I'm saying. "No matter what the test says. You can't live your life in fear, baby," I tell her, completely ignoring anyone else listening.

"Perfect, I'll call your mother, Deacon."

Brynn throws her mother a look, then leans her forehead against mine. "Do you realize what you've done?" she asks me, and her father laughs . . . hard.

"You've unleashed a kraken, son. Don't say you weren't warned." Cade pushes Sam's still-full glass of bourbon my way and holds his up, waiting for me to do the same. "Welcome to the family, Deacon."

BRYNLEE

**Deacon is the love of my life, but my tribe...
They're my soulmates.**

—Brynlee's Secret Thoughts

I wait a few days until Everly and Gracie are back with the guys from Maine before I send my text.

BRYNLEE

Any chance we could get everyone together tonight?

LINDY

Everyone, everyone? Like the guys and the kids? Or just the girls?

MADDOX

Am I supposed to be on this text?

BRYNLEE

Yes.

EVERLY

Ohh. You've been forgiven for Apartment-swap-gate?

CALLEN

Is that your attempt at turning this into Watergate?

KENZIE

Do you even know what Watergate was, Callen?

CALLEN

You don't need to be a doctor to know history, Kenz.

GRACIE

Who let them in here? I vote them off the island.

BRYNLEE

I included them, and yes, bring the guys and the kids.

GRACIE

We're not all fitting in the condo, Brynnie.

MADDOX

We'll all fit in ours though.

LINDY

Ohhh . . . Those are fighting words.

EVERLY

Shit. No throwing stuff in front of the kids. I don't need Jaxon throwing shit at his sister because he sees one of you do it. Got me?

BRYNLEE

No. Not the penthouse either. The lake house next to Jace's.

LINDY

Did you buy a house and not tell us, Brynn?

EVERLY

Holy shit! You did, didn't you?

MADDOX

Worse.

BRYNLEE

How do you know it's worse, Madman?

MADDOX

I'm like God. I know everything.

LINDY

More like the Wizard of Oz, pulling the strings behind the curtain. Impressive until you see who it really is.

MADDOX

Never heard any complaints when the curtain gets pulled.

KENZIE

I think I followed that innuendo, and I think I may have just vomited.

EVERLY

We've got to do something about your gag reflex, Kenz. It's getting worse.

CALLEN

I volunteer as tribute.

GRACIE

You are so gross.

CALLEN

This isn't new news, good twin.

KENZIE

Whatever. You better FaceTime me so I get to hear the news.

EVERLY

Wait. What does Maddox know that we don't, and why are we meeting at a lake house?

MADDOX

You want me to tell them, Brynnie?

BRYNLEE

I'll see you guys at seven. I'll order pizza and get beer.

CALLEN

Shit. She's feeding us and watering us. It must be bad.

EVERLY

Watering? What is wrong with you? Did Grandma drop you on your head as a baby?

GRACIE

No. I blame football. He's taken too many hits.

BRYNLEE

It's Deacon Kane's house.

LINDY

The new hockey coach, Deacon Kane?

EVERLY

What the hell?

GRACIE

Oh my God. He's who you were having sex with on the couch?

MADDOX

Seriously didn't need that visual.

CALLEN

I'm okay with it.

> GRACIE
> Too far, Callen.
>
> CALLEN
> No such thing.
>
> MADDOX
> Tell them or I will.

I look down at the screen, then kiss my husband before walking outside with a smile.

> BRYNLEE
> He's the man I married.

Then I power my phone down and relax before the chaos ensues later.

---

*I*n all fairness, they took the whole *I got married without them* thing pretty well.

I mean, I may have heard my fair share of jokes from Easton and Lindy about copying them, but they all came from a good place.

Now, as the sun sets and the kids run around in the grass, Deacon wraps his arms around me from behind and looks over at our guests, who are mostly sitting on the outdoor sectional, sipping wine and beer. Or in the twins' case, water. "I guess that was the easy part," I murmur, fortifying my nerves before I break the rest of my news to them.

THE SWEET SPOT

Deacon presses his lips to my temple. "You could wait until you get the results back."

"No. Our moms have managed to put a wedding together for us less than two weeks from now. I want to spend that time with the girls, finding dresses and picking flowers, and I don't want to hide anything else from them. I might need them more than ever, depending on the results." I close my eyes and soak in Deacon's strength. "I love you."

"You're the strongest woman I know, Brynlee Kane. You've got this."

"I haven't changed my name yet," I tease.

"But you will," he assures me, and he's right. I will.

We move over to where everyone is gathered.

This group of men and women, who in so many ways are every bit my family, some by blood but all by choice . . . These people mean the world to me.

"Hey guys," I clear my throat as we walk over and wait for the talking to stop.

"Ahh, hell. Are you pregnant too?" Lindy asks. "Someone get Kenzie on FaceTime because I can't deal with Everly, Gracie, and Brynlee all pregnant at the same time. I'm going to need reinforcements."

No sooner has she said it than Gracie holds up her phone with Kenzie's face, half asleep on the screen. "Got her."

"Umm . . . what?" Kenzie asks from what looks like behind a desk somewhere in the hospital.

"Brynlee's pregnant, Doc," Callen groans.

"I'm sorry, what did you just say?" Kenzie asks, clearly concerned.

"I'm not pregnant," I reassure everyone but especially Kenzie, since she's the only one besides Deacon and I who knows the potential complications that would come with that. "But I do need to tell you something."

The group quiets until all we hear is the kids' laughter as

Cross and Everly's daughter chases her brother and Lindy and Easton's son.

"So . . . I took a test this week," I tell them, while I try desperately to control the trembling in my voice. "I should have the results back in a few days. But I wanted you to know now. I wanted you all to be prepared for whatever the results are."

Callen moves to say something, but Gracie rests her hand on his, stopping him.

"I love you all so much, and I hate that I haven't told you before, but I had to come to terms with it on my own first," I tell them all, fighting back tears. "A few months ago, I found out my biological mother died from complications of Huntington's disease." I put my hand up and stop everyone from asking questions all at once. "In case you're not familiar with it, because lord knows I wasn't before all of this, yes, it's hereditary, and no, there's no cure."

I stop before I start to cry, and Deacon wraps his arms around me.

"If you've got questions, call me, and we'll talk later," Kenzie offers. "I'm proud of you for getting tested, Brynn."

"Now what?" Maddox asks, having not moved from his spot at the back of the group. "What can we do, Brynn?"

"Now, nothing. We get ready for a wedding ten days from now. Now Everly tailors my wedding dress tomorrow. Now we watch those beautiful babies smile while they make a mess of the cupcakes I picked up from Sweet Temptations earlier. Now we live, and we love, and we don't waste a single second—because life is too damn short."

I kiss Deacon's cheek and pull away, then make my way down to where Kerrigan is chasing Jax and Griffin and join in on the chase, needing a little bit of their beautiful innocence to wash away some of my grief right now.

Deacon

It feels like half my damn team is watching me once the girls close ranks around Brynn after her announcement. Easton Hayes, both Wilder brothers, and Nixon Sinclair all stand around with Brynn's cousin Maddox and Callen Sinclair rounding the group out. And right now, I don't give a shit about talking with any of them.

"You need anything, Coach?" Nix asks while the others give me space.

"A crystal ball would be nice," I tell him because what else am I supposed to say?

Yeah. I need my wife to be healthy.

I need her not to die.

I need a long lifetime with her.

But I don't tell him any of that. Brynlee is the only person who gets those words, so I settle for, "I need to know she's going to be okay, no matter what that test says."

"She will be," Easton Hayes, Lindy's husband and I think Brynn's cousin, if I'm following her fucked up family tree correctly, tells me. "You don't know that group of women yet, Coach. Individually, they're so fucking strong. But together . . . they're a sight to be seen."

Callen laughs a dry, emotionless sound. "Wait until you see them pissed off as a unit. I've never seen anything like it. They've got our girl."

"*My* girl," I correct him with a fucking scary note of possession in my voice that this motherfucker better hear.

"Your wife, Kane. But we all love her. She's been my

friend since we were three years old. That doesn't change because she's married. She'll always be my friend. They're all like sisters to us," he tells me, and I'm not sure if I want to hit him or not.

"Thank God, you're a good athlete, Callen, because you're a fucking shit communicator," Cross tells him as he watches his wife and kids down by the lake.

"Dude, you weren't there, Wilder. Maddox, Nix, and I were. Our whole lives have been intertwined with those women. Even Easton didn't come into the picture until middle school. I love them all like they're my damn sisters. That's all I'm trying to say."

Ares elbows Callen. "Dude, I'd just stop. No man wants to hear you love his wife—myself included."

"Jesus Christ, your wife is my niece, for fuck's sake," Callen snaps back, and my head swims.

"The fuck?" I ask. "Are all you fuckers related in this goddamn town?"

"Pretty much," Cross answers.

Maddox hands me a beer. "You'll get used to it."

I stare at him, remembering what Brynn told me when we were at her parents' house. "Your dad is Sam, right?"

Maddox sips his beer. "Yup."

"He might be the first man I've ever been scared of," I tell him with a little humility.

"Dude, you should meet his mom," Nix laughs, but more importantly, Brynlee's laugh floats up to me from the shoreline, where the girls are kicking water at the toddlers.

"You guys can all love her, but she's mine."

*O*nce everyone leaves, I go on the hunt for my wife.

I should have known she'd be outside, sitting in an Adirondak chair down by the lake. A soft, white blanket is wrapped around her, while she's staring up at the stars with a peaceful look on her face.

She tilts her head up to me once she hears me coming. "Hey."

"Hey, baby." I scoop her up, then sit down with her in my lap. "How are you feeling?"

"Like I've been run over by a tractor trailer," she tells me, then rests her head against my chest. "Tonight was a lot."

"Yeah. It was. What you did took strength, Brynn. So much strength." I run my hand up and down her back, enjoying the feel of her in my arms. "You've got a lot of people who love you."

"Yeah," she agrees softly. "I do."

"I thought I was going to have to kill Callen Sinclair there for a minute." Fucker will never know how close he came to eating my fist.

"What?" She pops her head up, confusion visible on every inch of her beautiful face.

"He tried to tell me how much everyone loves you, but it came out sounding like he was in love with you." I lean my head back against the chair and watch the laughter dance in her emerald-green eyes.

"Nothing to worry about there, husband. He's like a brother to me. They all are."

"They're all protective of you, baby. You've got a good group of friends around you. People who want to be here for you. By the end of the night, everyone had pulled me aside to make sure I had their numbers. They all told me to take care of you. They all told me to call if I needed anything. I'm pretty sure Easton had to drag Lindy out of here because at one point, I think she wanted to spend the night." I tuck her hair behind her ear and twirl the strands around my finger. "He told me they live down the street, Brynn, and she didn't want to leave you."

She smiles softly and lays her head on my shoulder, quietly taking it all in.

"I guess what I'm trying to say is you are loved, Brynlee Kane. You have so many people in your corner, and no matter what the test results say, you're going to be okay." I press my lips against her head and breathe her in. Committing this moment to memory. Holding her here, just like this, with the fireflies dancing over the lake and the falls in the distance drowning out the world. I fell in love with her in this lake.

"You sure you don't want to just get married here, Brynn?"

"No," she whispers without lifting her head. "I want to marry you on Block Island. It's where our story starts."

"It's a pretty great story, red." I struggle to hold back the tears burning the backs of my eyes. "And we've got a whole lot of chapters still to write."

Her body shakes when she loses the battle with her own tears.

"I guess it's a good thing the length of the story isn't what makes it good," she tells me as she wipes her face. "It's how you fill those pages that matters."

She turns and sets a tear-filled smile on me. "Promise me we'll fill every last one. No matter how long our book ends up being. Promise me we'll make every page count. Every word count. Even if it's shorter than we expected. It will be the sweetest love story ever told."

It takes me a long time to answer her, not because I don't want to agree, but because I can't get the damn words out.

When I lose the fight with my composure, and the first

damn tear falls, I blow out a deep breath, but I can't give her what she wants. "You promise me it's going to be a really long book, Brynn. I don't want it to be short. I want it to be a sweeping epic."

Brynlee wipes the tears from my cheeks. "I can't make you that promise, Deacon. You know I can't.

"You have to. I want vacations and Christmas mornings. Hockey games and proms. I want Thanksgivings with your whole fucked up family because something tells me they're pretty epic. I want more kids, Brynn, and I want you to be there the day Kennedy gets married. I want it all, baby, and I want it with you. You have to promise me you'll be there for all of it, Brynlee. No matter what some stupid test tells us, you have to promise you'll fight for us. You won't give up. You won't hide. You'll fight."

"I'm scared I won't be enough, Deacon," she admits on a sob.

"You already are, baby. And when you're tired of the fight, I'll fight for you." She buries her face against my chest as tears rack her beautiful body, and I hold her, knowing it's out of our hands. All that's left to do is wait.

𝕿𝖍𝖊 𝕻𝖍𝖎𝖑𝖑𝖞 𝕻𝖗𝖊𝖘𝖘

KROYDON KRONICLES

A ROYAL AFFAIR

It may have taken me some time to confirm this scoop, but when it's this big, a reporter has to triple check her sources. And this one is the biggest of big, giant, juicy scoops we've had in a long time. Think *triple chocolate fudge sundae with all the toppings* big.

Kroydon Hills' newest, hottest hockey coach, Deacon Kane, did not waste any time marrying into our own royal family. You heard it first here, ladies and gentlemen. Deacon Kane put a ring on Brynlee St. James's finger. These socialites just can't keep their hands off some of our favorite hockey pucks. Rumor has it, the first event was an intimate affair, but the Kingston family has left Kroydon Hills to celebrate in a way only the Kingstons can.

Stay tuned for all the dirty deets.

#KroydonKronicles #PuckPack #PuckingWifes

BRYNLEE

"Seriously, we don't all leave until tomorrow. How do they find this shit out?" Everly bitches as she puts the finishing touches on the train of my dress in her boutique a few days later.

"Don't get too pissed when you have pins near my ass, please," I beg as Lindy and Gracie sit with my mom, sipping champagne, though in Gracie's case, it's apple juice.

"Do you need any help," my mom asks Kennedy gently from the other side of the dressing room door.

After a moment, a quiet, "No thanks," answers back.

This all came together too quickly for Isla to change her travel arrangements, so she left two days ago. And while Kennedy has opened up to me pretty quickly, the rest of the family can be overwhelming on the best of days. And she hasn't had to deal with all of them yet. Luckily, Deacon said Kennedy's favorite place in the world is his parents' inn, so we're hoping that helps.

She walks out a minute later in a white dress with mint-green trim and a mint-green sash, her dark hair pulled back from her face and a deer-in-the-headlights look in her eyes.

"No heels, right? I don't want to fall on my face in front of a ton of people."

"Kit Kat . . . you look beautiful," I tell her with awe in my voice.

She ignores everyone else in the room, focusing solely on me, which I think helps her, then she stops next to me. "You look like a princess, Brynnie."

Mom makes a noise that makes us all stop and turn.

"Ignore me," she insists as she wipes her eyes. "You'll all understand one day when your babies get married."

"I'm never getting married," Kennedy tells me. "Boys are stupid and annoying."

"Amen, sister," Kenzie tells her through the FaceTime call the girls have set up so she can be here for this since she can't get off for the wedding. "We don't need men, Kennedy."

"Oh, but they're so much fun," Lindy laughs, and my mom shakes her head.

Gracie reaches inside my bag and grabs my vibrating phone. "Your phone is ringing, Brynn."

I take the phone from her and see my doctor's name.

"Go get Deacon, Grace. He's next door at Sweet Temptations. Please go get him." I look from Mom to Kennedy and fight back my fear. We've kept this from her on purpose, not wanting to worry her until we have to.

I answer the call quickly, not wanting it to go to voicemail and watching the confusion fill Kennedy's eyes. "Hi, Dr. Ambrosano. Can you give me just a minute? I'm standing in the middle of a room being fitted for my wedding gown."

"Sure, Brynlee. I'm going to put you on hold and jump on this next call. I'll be back in less than five minutes."

I take a deep breath. "Thank you."

"Kennedy, you look perfect. How about you get changed and go with Lindy next door to get a cupcake? Would that be okay?"

Her big golden eyes see way more than she lets on as she nods her head. "Are you okay, Brynlee?"

"I will be, honey. Don't worry about me." I turn to Everly and plaster on the fakest smile of my life. "Can you please get me out of this dress before Deacon gets up here?"

"Pretty sure it's not bad luck if you've already married the groom, Brynn," she whispers, then shuts up when I throw a glare her way.

By the time Deacon gets here, I'm sitting on a couch in Everly's office in a silk robe with the phone on speaker and horrible elevator music filling the room.

His wild eyes catch mine as he squats down in front of me, and my mom and dad walk into the room, carefully closing the door behind them.

"You brought the whole family," I laugh halfheartedly.

"I called your father when Grace went to go get Deacon," Mom offers, and I see my dad take her hand in his.

"Your brother is waiting outside the door," Dad tells me, and I notice the gym clothes and tape on his hands. I guess he was working with Killian when Mom called.

"Miss St. James," Dr. Ambrosano says as the music cuts off abruptly. "Sorry to keep you waiting."

"It's actually Mrs. Kane now," I tell her, looking at my handsome husband, who has his hands resting on my hips as he watches my every breath.

"We received the results of your test, Mrs. Kane." An entire lifetime passes in the seconds before she speaks again. "They came back negative."

She keeps talking, but as my face falls to Deacon's chest, I don't hear a word past *negative*, and it may be the most beautiful word I've ever heard. The phone falls from my fingers, and I throw my arms around Deacon's neck and let him take all my weight.

He lifts me from my feet and holds me so damn tight, I'm

surprised I can still breathe, but I don't want him to ever let go. "She said negative, right?" I ask through the tears, and my husband shakes his head as he cries tears of joy.

He kisses me so damn hard, I may never breathe again. Like he's proving to us both I'm alive and right here in his arms. "She said negative, baby. She said negative," he repeats, like a sacred vow falling from his lips. "You're going to have a long life, Brynlee Kane. We're going to fill every single page with the best life you could ever imagine."

I press my lips to his tears. "The sweetest story, Deacon."

"Our story, Brynlee."

Our story.

BRYNLEE

You deserve the kind of love that brings peace to your soul.

—Brynlee's Secret Thoughts

"What are you doing down here, Brynn?"

I look up at Maddox and smile as I enjoy the Atlantic Ocean washing over my feet. "It's beautiful out here, isn't it?"

"Yeah." He looks out at the dark waves. "I guess it is. You doing okay?"

"Why wouldn't I be?" I hip-check him gently. "Because I'm standing in the ocean, alone, the night before my wedding?"

"Well yeah, I guess. The girls are all up at the inn. Pretty sure Deacon is sitting in the dining room, enjoying a bottle of very old, very expensive bourbon with our dads. I heard our sisters saying they were going into town to see if they could find a little trouble. Have I told you how damn glad I am that Livvy didn't go to the same school as Caitlin? Jesus. Those two together scare the shit out of me," he admits, and a laugh burst from my lips.

He's not wrong.

Those two are dangerous together.

"What are you talking about? Nothing scares you, Madman." I kick water at his ankles and soak his rolled-up pants.

"You scared the shit out of me, Brynnie. You're the heart of us all. You know that, right? You're the nucleus. The one who holds us all together. The one who brought the twins into our craziness as kids. Who then brought Callen with them. The girls played soccer because you did. I trained at Crucible because I couldn't have my girl cousin be a better fighter than me. You lead. We follow. Nothing can happen to you." He shoves his hands in his pockets, then looks away.

"Maddox . . . that's not true," I protest.

"It is. I'm a lot of things, but a liar isn't one of them." His hoarse voice almost scares me. I've never seen him like this.

"I'm okay. The test came back negative. You know this. Everyone knows." I grab his arm and make him look at me. "I don't lie either. I'm fine."

"Yeah. I guess I just wanted to hear you say it." He wraps an arm around my shoulders and tilts his head against mine. "Guess you can't be mad at me about the condo switch anymore since you've already moved out of ours and into Deacon's house."

"You fucker," I giggle. "I guess if I can forgive my mom for the job switch thing, I can forgive you for the condo swap too."

"Oh yeah? You let Scarlet off the hook?" he teases.

"It seemed pretty insignificant in light of everything else.

Besides, what does she always say?" I ask, without a doubt in my mind he knows the answer.

"Everything happens for a reason," Maddox murmurs with a shake of his head.

"Yup. Me working for Crucible makes my new life work so much better. I can be there for Kennedy when Deacon has to travel. My schedule will be much more flexible than it would have been." Mom likes to say we may never know the reason, but she fully believes there always is one. I think this is one of those rare times I have no doubt what the reason is. Because I had already made up my mind about leaving the Revolution, I didn't have to decide between my job and my family.

My family.

I love the sound of that.

"Yeah, I guess life has a funny way of working out, doesn't it?" Maddox's voice changes, and I look at him. Really look.

"Are you okay, Madman?"

"Brynnie?" I turn toward the voice calling my name and scream when I see Kenzie running my way.

"Kenzie? Oh my God. How are you here?" I shriek as she jumps, nearly tackling me into the ocean.

"Seriously, I can't even appreciate the two of you dry humping in front of me because we're all related. I need to move to a city where we don't have any fucking family," he grumbles.

"We love you too, Madman," Kenzie squeals, and he kicks water at us before he walks away.

"How are you here, Kenz?" I ask, once we both stop squeezing each other.

"I traded shifts with someone, and Becket sent a plane for me. I fly back tomorrow night. You didn't think I was going to miss your wedding, did you?"

"Well yeah, Kenz. I kinda did. You work sixty-hour work

weeks. You only get two days off a month." I link my pinky with hers and turn when I hear voices behind me to find the girls are walking down the beach. "Did you all know?"

They nod and admit they were in on the surprise.

"My heart feels so full it could burst right now, guys." The stupid tears I can't seem to stop start building behind my eyes.

"Kenz, is that like a medical condition or something?" Everly asks, and Gracie laughs.

"A bursting heart? Could you imagine?" Gracie shoves her sister with a smile.

"I mean, I'd be a goner because, Kenz, the way my heart feels like it's going to burst every time your brother gives me an orgasm . . . seriously, it would be bad." Lindy moves next to Kenzie and squeezes the hell out of her. "Can't you finish your residency in Philly? We miss you."

"You know I can't. Just don't have all your babies right away so I can deliver a few." Kenzie rubs the tiny little baby bump Everly has before she looks back at Lindy. "Everyone except you. No more sex with my brother. No more babies for you. If I have to hear you talk about death by dick one more time, I might never be able to look at you again."

"No can do, Kenz. He already made me come twice today."

"How?" I ask.

"Well, let's see, Brynn . . . when a man loves a woman," Everly starts, and I splash her.

"I know that, Evie. I meant, how, as in, we've been together all day."

"Morning sex is a lot of fun," Gracie announces with such a dreamy look on her face, I have to stop and stare. "How much sex were you and the god of war having in the room next to mine? I just have to ask."

"So much sex." She puts her finger up to her lips, like it's a secret, and Lindy pushes her out of the way and moves in front of me.

"Oh, young padawan. Welcome to motherhood, where you get it in *whenever* you can, *wherever* you can. You're going to learn to get creative really quickly now. My advice for a good marriage is that communication is key. If you think you guys are talking enough, talk some more. There can never be too much communication or too much sex. Plenty of sex is the other part of the advice. Get it in as much as possible. It doesn't always have to take hours either." I can't stop laughing as Kenzie turns a little green. "Oh, and drop to your knees every now and then. They fucking love that."

"Too far, Lindy. Too damn far." Kenzie shakes with laughter. "I missed you guys so much. I'm so jealous that you're all so in love and having great sex."

Lindy hugs her. "One day, you'll have great sex too, Kenz."

"Will it happen before I'm thirty?" she moans, and Lindy shrugs.

"Find a hot doctor and jump his bones in the on-call room like they do in *Grey's Anatomy*," Everly adds.

"It's not like that," Kenzie tells us and wraps her arm around my waist. "Let's have a slumber party like we used too."

"I call dibs on the bed." Lindy links her arm around Kenzie's waist, and the twins do the same thing on the other side of me.

"I love you ladies," I tell them all. "Thank you for being my family."

"Soulmates," Gracie says.

"Soulmates," I agree.

And at three a.m., when I can't sleep because five grown women in one bed is four too many, I find myself knocking on my husband's door.

It takes him a hot minute to get the door open. And when

THE SWEET SPOT

he does, he's shirtless with just a pair of black boxer briefs covering his very impressive body, and I'm reminded of one of the many reasons I love this man. "God, you're gorgeous," I tell him as I wrap my arms around his neck and my legs around his waist.

He shuts the door behind us and presses me up against it. "I thought we weren't supposed to see each other before the wedding. Isn't it bad luck?" he growls as he licks inside my mouth, setting every inch of my body on fire.

"Yeah well, I'm supposed to be a virgin too. Let's not get caught up in what we're supposed to do, husband." I grind down against his beautifully hard cock and moan. "Lock the door in case Kennedy comes looking for you," I murmur against his lips and shove his boxers down with my feet as he locks the door and crosses the room.

Deacon sits down on the bed and runs his hands up my legs, dragging up the long white cotton nightgown I just bought with his hands. "I like this, baby. It's all sweet and innocent."

He doesn't take it off me, just finds the strings of my lace panties and rips them from my body.

So fucking hot.

Deacon's mouth is hot and firm, and it's everywhere.

My neck. My shoulders. My ears.

"What do you want, wife?" he growls before biting down on my earlobe.

I reach between us and wrap my hand around his dick and pump him. "I want to come on your cock, husband."

"You want it slow and sweet, baby?" He runs a finger through my sex and around my clit before he plunges it inside me.

"No," I cry out at the invasion. "I want you to fuck me. Hard and fast. Make me come, then hold me while I sleep."

He pulls out and plunges two fingers deep inside me,

curling them and scraping that rough patch only he's ever found, and I throw my head back and moan. "Fuck, that feels so good."

"Give me one now, Brynn." He takes my breast in his mouth and bites down on my nipple as he repeats that incredible thing he does with his fingers, and that's all it takes. I come fast and hard and so damn much, I'm surprised his hand doesn't cramp while he works me through my first orgasm.

"That's one, baby." He lifts me from his lap, then lays me down on the bed and tugs my nightgown off me, then kicks his boxer briefs off and drags me to the edge of the bed. "This is going to be two, Mrs. Kane."

He drops to his fucking knees for me and spreads my pussy. One finger runs through my drenched sex, and I squirm and bend my knees and plant my feet flat against the bed. "Deacon..."

"Patience, Brynn. I'm going to give you what you need. But I'm taking what I want first." He kisses his way up the inside of my thigh, leaving goosebumps all over my flesh. He throws my legs over his shoulder, leaving me at his mercy, and pulls my ass right up to the edge of the bed before he finally... finally, drags his tongue up the length of my pussy, then sucks my clit between his lips.

"Ohmygod," I scream, already overstimulated from my first orgasm.

He tongues me over and over, adding one thick finger, then another until I'm a quivering, needy mess, and thank God, I don't know whose rooms are on either side of this one because there's no way the walls can hide my screams.

I grind shamelessly against his face, my heels digging into his back, and my husband growls his approval against my pussy until I'm quivering and shattering again. Only this time, he doesn't wait for my orgasm to stop before he puts a knee on the bed and notches his cock against my core. My mouth waters and opens, but no sound comes out as he fills me in one fast, deliciously hard thrust, stealing my breath from my body.

"That's my greedy girl. You gonna show me how bad you want my cock?" He drops his body down over mine, giving me his weight the way I love, and presses his lips to mine, pushing his tongue into my mouth and forcing me to taste myself on him. It's so damn hot.

His strong hands grip my hips and rolls us over so I'm on top. But in no way am I in control. Deacon sits up, bringing us chest to chest and wraps an arm around me, holding my head in his hand. He pulls my hair back and pushes his hips up, nice and slow. "Is this what you want, wife?" he taunts me, and fuck, it's so hot.

He moves me like a rag doll. Dragging every inch of his decadent cock inside me.

Filling me until I feel like I can't possibly take anymore.

I circle my arms around his neck and lift my hips, then slam them back down on him. Taking him even deeper. Pushing us both higher." Deacon . . ." I gasp in warning. "I'm so close."

"I've got you, baby," he growls against my mouth, and my God, the way my body knows this man. His words are just as hot as his body.

He shifts and changes the angle just enough that I see stars.

"Deacon—" I call out as I shake.

He keeps up his slow pace. Brutally slow.

Dragging out every single second.

Wringing every ounce of pleasure from my body before he empties himself inside me in one final thrust. "My fucking wife."

When I swing my legs off the bed a few hours later, Deacon's arm wraps around my waist like a vice and drags me back to him, spooning me. "Where are you going?" he rasps in a sexy, sleepy voice.

"I have to get back to my room before anyone comes looking for me," I whimper as his hand moves to my breast. "No more, Deacon. I can't. You have to wait until tonight or I won't be able to walk down the aisle." I'm only half kidding. He made me come two more times in as many hours, and five is a new record for us.

He pulls the blanket up over us and buries his face in my hair. "I married you so I could wake up with you every day."

"You married me because you needed a wife," I tease and roll over in his arms and press my lips to his chin. "Now you have to marry me again in front of both our families in a few hours, and it takes this girl a lot of time to get ready, so you're going to have to let go."

He drags his eyes over my face. "Marrying you was the best thing I ever did, Brynn."

"Well, if you want to do it again in a few hours, you've got to let me go." This man is everything I never knew I needed. "Don't forget this whole thing was your idea."

"Yeah well, your parents like me now, and don't think for one minute your dad getting to walk you down the aisle didn't help get us out of the doghouse." He takes my mouth in the most sinful kiss, and for one single hot second, I consider staying right here in this bed.

"I'll see you in a few hours, Mr. Kane. I'll be the one in white." I pull away and commit this moment to my memory.

"Wait." He sits up and pulls something out of the drawer in the nightstand. "Here. It's just a little wedding present."

It's wrapped in white paper with a golden ribbon tied around it, and I'm pretty sure he wrapped it himself, judging by the looks of it.

"I didn't get you anything." I turn it over in my hands, guilt building that it didn't even cross my mind.

"You already gave me my gift, Brynn. You're here, standing in front of me." He shrugs almost shyly. "Open it."

"Okay," I agree, kind of enjoying this less confident version of Deacon. I carefully untie the ribbon, making sure I don't rip the paper yet. I want to take my time. This is the first gift Deacon's ever given me. I slide my finger under the tape and pull away the paper, then look at the plain brown leather notebook in my hand and flip it over.

On the front is a monogram.

DKB.

Our monogram.

And the month and year we came to Block Island all those years ago is engraved in the leather beneath it.

"Deacon . . ." My words die in my mouth, and I drop down on the bed next to him.

"It's when our story started," he tells me with his chin resting on my shoulder. "I thought maybe you'd want to fill it with all our adventures."

"It's the most perfect thing anyone has ever given me." I bite down on my lip, completely overwhelmed.

"You're the most perfect thing I've ever been given, Brynn," he tells me, and I very carefully place the book on the nightstand. "What are you doing?"

I pull my nightgown back over my head. "It's not like they can start the wedding without us."

His smile is so damn sexy. "No, baby, it's not. But it'll be a funny chapter."

"Maybe we don't let anyone else ever read this book, okay?" I push back on his shoulders and run my fingers over his lips. "I love you."

"Until the very end, Brynn."

"Until the very end, Deacon."

BRYNLEE

And they lived happily ever after...

—Brynlee's Secret Thoughts

I watch my mother attach my veil through the reflection of the antique mirror in the bridal suite. She's trying hard not to cry, but the woman the world likes to call an ice queen is struggling.

"Don't cry, Mom. It'll ruin your makeup." I smile back at her as she sucks in a shaky breath.

"Look out. She's gonna cry now," my little sister teases, and oh boy, am I glad I'm not on the receiving end of the glare Mom just threw her way.

"Zip it, you," Mom warns Livvy while Gracie and Everly laugh. "Can you three give us a minute?"

As the door closes behind them, I turn to face my mother. This woman I've wanted to emulate my whole life. And I'm suddenly tongue-tied, trying to tell her how I feel.

"Mom . . ."

"Shh . . . I know," she whispers as she fluffs my dress out around me and dabs the corners of her own eye with a tissue. "You, my darling girl, are the most beautiful thing I've ever seen in my life, and I'm so incredibly proud of the woman you've become." She gently moves my hair behind my shoulders, then adjusts my veil once more before she smiles. "I'd like to think I had a little something to do with that. Thank you for letting me be your mother." Her voice catches, and she purses her lips as she tries to hold back her tears. "I love you."

My lips tremble, and my eyes fill as I wave my hand in front of my face, trying to stop my tears from falling.

If they start now, they won't stop.

"Now you're going to make me cry. Stop," I plead lovingly before stepping into her arms and holding her as if my life depended on it, like I used to do when I was a little girl. "There was never a better mother than you," I manage to get out before someone knocks on the door.

"It's time, Brynn," my dad calls out. "Can I come in?"

I look back at my mom, suddenly nervous. "Do I look okay?"

She nods with a trembling smile. "You look beautiful, baby," she manages to get out before opening the door for my dad and whispering something to him before he walks in, as handsome as ever in his tux.

"Brynlee," he whispers reverently. "You've never looked more beautiful."

"Thank you, Daddy."

He takes my hands in his and swallows. "I love all my children equally. But you and me, kid. We're special in a way they can't understand. Not your mom or your brother and sister. It was just you and me for a long time. You taught me what unconditional love is. You helped shape the man I am. And now you get to do that for Deacon too."

I look up at the ceiling, trying desperately to get my emotions in check.

"He's a good man, Brynn. And he loves you. I couldn't ask for anything more for my baby. Now humor your old man, and let me give you just a few words of wisdom, okay?"

I nod, unable to form words.

"Never go to bed angry. I know everyone says that, but it's cliché for a reason. Choose your battles. If it really matters, fight for it. If it doesn't, don't. Never be mean. Even when you're mad at each other. And never use your love as a bargaining chip. It's not a tool. It's the greatest gift in the world. Remember that."

He takes my face in his hands and gently presses his lips against the top of my head. "And don't make the man come to every family function if he doesn't feel like it. Most of the world didn't grow up with as big of a family as you were blessed with, kid. It's a little overwhelming for those of us who weren't born into this chaos. Give him a pass every now and then."

He wipes a tear from my cheek. "Don't cry, baby. Your mother will kill me."

"Thank you, Daddy. For everything."

"I love you, Brynlee. Now, let's go before one of your uncles decides to take the microphone away from the judge who's waiting to marry you." He links my arm through his. "You ready?"

I look at the first man I ever loved and suddenly understand why a father gives a daughter away. He's giving me to the last man I'll ever love.

"I'm ready."

Deacon

"You nervous, brother?' Rip asks from next to me at the end of the aisle.

"Not even a little," I tell him as the music changes and Kenndy appears at the end of the aisle. She looks petrified, but my brave girl smiles at me and keeps her eyes focused only on me as she walks down the aisle. She kisses my cheek when she makes it to me.

"I did what you said, Dad. I never looked away," she tells me, so damn proud of herself.

"I love you, Kennedy. Do you want to stand up here with me?" I ask, even though I know the answer.

"Not a chance," she whispers and fist-bumps Rip. "I'm going to go sit with Grandma and Grandpa."

By the time the music changes to an instrumental version of "Here Comes The Sun," I'm ready to march down the aisle to Brynlee myself. But then Cade and she round the corner, and I get my first glance of my wife. My beautiful wife. Every single moment in my life has led me here, and I'd gladly go through it all again to get to spend my life with this woman.

She and Cade stop in front of me, and he lifts her veil and kisses her cheek before putting her hand in mine. "Take care of my baby girl, Deacon."

"With my life, Cade."

Brynn hands her sister her bouquet and places her other hand in mine. "Are you ready for our next chapter, Deacon?"

"Our next of many, Brynn." I cup her face in my hand and press my lips to hers.

The judge clears his throat and everyone around us laughs. "We're not quite there yet, Deacon."

Brynn's eyes sparkle like the Fourth of July.

"We've been there for a long time, haven't we, baby?" I whisper, and she smiles the most beautiful smile.

"Our story started here," she whispers.

Yeah. Our story started here.

EPILOGUE I

DEACON

Most people would never believe the way the chemistry in a team can be made or broken in a locker room. Games are won and lost in here every day.

My team has been on fire all postseason.

I couldn't ask for more, but I'm about to.

"We've got one period left, men. Twenty minutes stand between you and accomplishing the goal you set for yourselves the first fucking time you laced up your skates. For some of you, this is your last chance. For others, it might be your *only* chance. I've never held Lord Stanley's Cup, but I fucking want to. Twenty minutes, men . . . Twenty minutes . . . Now go make yourself immortal."

Jace and I lead the men through the tunnel, then stand aside as my team of warriors skate out onto the ice. "That was a really good one, Coach," Jace tells me with a smile. "Hell, I want to be immortal, and my name is engraved on that thing already."

"Fuck off, Kingston." I smack his arm with my clipboard, and we walk into the box together.

I had no clue the ways my life would change when the

Kingstons offered me this job, but as I look up at the box above me where my wife and daughter sit, surrounded by our friends and family, I can't help but think what a lucky fucker I am.

My life is good, whether we win this thing or not.

But goddamn, I want to win it so bad, I can taste it.

And twenty minutes later, as the clock ticks down on the last three seconds of the game, we're tied 1–1, when Nixon Sinclair takes a slapshot from more than halfway down center ice that sails right past Montreal's goalie. The buzzer rings as time runs out, and the entire stadium erupts around us.

"Holy shit." Jace jumps, and our entire bench empties as my players all make their way to Nixon. "They fucking did it. I can't believe they fucking did it."

"Coach Kane," a reporter from ESPN calls out to me, already rushing the ice. "Coach Kane, do you have any comment on how it feels to win your first championship, making you the youngest head coach in history to win it?"

I look up into the box to see if I can spot Brynlee and Kennedy, but everyone is on their feet celebrating, and I don't see them.

"Coach Kane, any comments for the doubters who said your team couldn't pull a repeat?"

I turn and look out at my team celebrating on the ice.

Do I have any words?

"They earned it. That's all I have to say right now. I'll see you in the press conference shortly," I tell the growing crowd as a carpet is laid out on the ice for us to walk on. Cross Wilder, our team captain, is already taking a lap with the Cup when I make it out to my guys, having been stopped every few feet by another reporter.

"Coach," Nixon calls out before he hugs me. "We fucking did it, Coach."

"We fucking did, Nix. That was a beautiful shot. Had to be close to a hundred and fifty feet."

"Yeah well, I guess I wanted immortality, Coach."

I look around at the confetti falling from the ceiling and the entire arena on their feet. "Pretty sure you got it, Nix. Good job."

"Coach Kane," a voice in the crowd I would know anywhere calls out.

I turn around and watch my wife walk up to me in her Revolution jersey she had specially made for her and Kennedy. They both have *Kane* across the back, and for the number, Kennedy's says ½, while Brynlee's says *00*. God, I love my wife.

She throws her arms around my neck, and I pull her against me. "Congratulations, Coach Kane," she teases me. "I've got a couple of ideas of ways we can celebrate tonight."

"And my day keeps getting better," I tell her. "Any chance one of them involves you in nothing but this jersey, red?"

"Oh, there's a very good chance of that happening." Brynlee presses her lips to mine, and I tuck her against me as I look around at this ragtag group that's somehow become my family.

Before the end of the night, someone manages to snap a picture that I make a mental note to get hold of and have framed for my wife. It's the two of us with Gracie and Ares and their newborns, Jake and Molly, standing next to Cross and Everly and their baby girl, Tennyson, and Jaxon and Kerrigan standing in front of them. Lindy and Easton are behind us, with Griffin sitting on his father's shoulders, and Nixon is squatting down next to Kennedy, who's holding the Cup in front of her. Ares wanted to put Jake in the Cup, but Gracie told him not unless it was sanitized first.

"A year ago, did you ever think you'd be standing here, Deacon?" Brynlee asks me before we finally leave the ice.

"Not in my wildest dreams, Brynn." I pull a piece of confetti out of her hair and hand it to her. "Here. In case you want it for the book."

"Good idea." She carefully puts it in her pocket and smiles.

That leather notebook I gave her has become a scrapbook of sorts. I've watched her put cards in there. She also prints out pictures and sticks them in there, every now and then. And every once in a while, she reads me something she wrote in there. "Are you ready for our next adventure?"

I run my fingers through her hair and tug. Our next adventure is three weeks in Japan, visiting Isla and Shaun, and if Kennedy is comfortable, we're going to leave her there with Isla for a month. Then Isla will fly home with her and spend a few weeks in the States before she flies back, though I promised Brynn she wouldn't be staying with us. "Am I ready for our next adventure?" I look around at my unbelievable life and count my blessings. "Yeah, baby. I'm ready."

"Love you, Coach Kane."

"Till the very end, Brynn . . . Till the very end."

EPILOGUE II

BRYNLEE

Three years later

"Have I told you how happy I am that you're joining Wren's practice, Kenz?" I ask as I shove the heel of my palm into the foot my son is currently kicking me with. Deacon likes to joke that when our son is born, he's going to be a hockey player, but I don't know. The way this kid is kicking me, I'm thinking I may have a future MMA champion on my hands.

She leans her head back against her beach chair and looks at me through giant sunglasses. "It feels so good to be done with my residency. I just want to feel like I'm finally starting my life instead of watching it pass me by."

"Well, I'm glad you're taking a month down here before you start working. You deserve a break, Kenz." Lindy pushes her sunglasses up on top of her head and smiles out at Griffin, who's jumping waves in the ocean, while Easton holds their baby girl curled up like a ball against his chest, her giant white sun hat shading her sleeping face. "I swear I'm not saying this on purpose, but seriously I can't look at my husband holding our daughter without getting all sorts of turned-on."

"Oh. My. God. Madeline. What is wrong with you?" Kenzie practically shouts at Lindy, and all the guys in the ocean turn to stare at us.

"Once we get you properly dicked, you'll understand, Kenz," Lindy assures her, and I want to die on Kenzie's behalf.

Gracie walks our way with Molly holding her hand. "What the heck are you guys yelling about?" she asks as she adjusts Molly's long-sleeved rash guard.

"Cover your ears, Molly, honey," Lindy tells her, then smiles at Gracie, who shakes her head before Lindy even speaks.

"Lindy, don't—"

"We were talking about getting Kenzie some good dick, now that she's got some time on her hands."

"Oh lord. You went there." Grace squats down in front of her daughter. "What did I tell you about repeating things you hear?"

"Not to," Molly's sweet voice repeats, proud of herself and her answer. She high-fives her mom.

"Good job, baby. Never repeat anything you hear your aunts say." She swats Molly's butt. "Now go play on the blanket. I'll be there in a minute."

Gracie watches Molly run to the blanket where Kennedy is reading *Little Women* for the hundredth time, and Everly and Tennyson are napping, then she sits in the empty chair next to me and leans forward to look down the line at Kenzie. "Are we talking about one dick in particular, or will any dick do? Because there's this single dad who brings his daughter to Molly's baby ballerina class, and he's hot. And his hands are huge."

I push my sunglasses up on top of my head and watch my husband body surf with Jace's twins. "I bet his hands aren't as big as Deacon's."

"Dude, Deacon's hands are huge. But we're not talking about your husband's porn-star dick," Lindy laughs.

"Umm, I'd rather hear about how hung he is. At least he's not my brother." Kenzie grabs Lindy's sunglasses off her head and tosses them in the waves as they pull back into the ocean.

"You did not," Lindy gasps, and the rest of us laugh.

"Fuck his brains out, Lindy. But for God's sake, stop telling me," Kenzie half laughs, half pleads while the rest of us practically roll out of our seats, dying from laughter. Finally, when we can all breathe again, Kenzie sticks her feet in the water and lays her seat all the way back. "I missed you bitches like I'd miss a limb, you know that, right?"

"It's good to have you home, Mackenzie," Lindy tells her as she squeezes her hand.

"Love you, ladies," I add to our little lovefest. A sniffle comes from Gracie's chair. "Are you crying?"

"Ignore me," she cries, and Kenzie kicks her feet in the water in front of her.

"You're pregnant?" Kenzie cries out, and all the men in the ocean turn again, this time to see which of their wives just got called out.

Only Ares is smiling from ear to ear.

Gracie nods her head super dramatically.

Oh no . . .

"I saw Wren last week."

"And," Kenzie pushes.

Grace sips from her water bottle as the color drains from her face. "And it's triplets."

*D*eacon crawls into bed that night and presses a kiss to my huge belly.

Of course, this kid is going to be a ten pounder. Because it doesn't worry me at all that they're already talking about his size, and I still have three months to go.

"How are you feeling, red?" He rolls over and drags me against his chest, just where I like to be.

"Tired but happy." I trace my finger over his pecs. "I'm not sure how I'm going to have the energy to travel to Killian's fight next month."

"Don't go," he tells me, like it's that simple.

"It's my job, Deacon. I have to go. Besides. I want to be there to watch him defend his title." Working for Crucible is everything I always hoped it would be. And with Deacon coaching the Revolution, I'm still as much a part of the team I love as I ever was. Just in a different capacity.

"What if I asked you not to go?" He presses, and I sit up very slowly because nothing I do at this point happens fast. Well almost nothing. Apparently, orgasms happen much faster when I'm pregnant. If I thought the sex was earth-shattering before, I have a whole new definition for that now. Damn. Seriously, I might be willing to have a whole hockey team of kids if this is how good it can be.

I force myself back to the current conversation and away from my husband's ability to screw me senseless.

"You wouldn't ask me not to go because you know how much my job means to me," I remind him with a hint of warning in my voice.

"I wouldn't. We agreed you'd stop at eight months. I'm

not trying to renegotiate now. I just worry about you, baby. You're tired already, and you're talking about flying to Vegas. I don't love it." He holds his arm up, and I slide back into place.

"I know. But the season won't have started yet, so you'll be with me, and Kennedy will be with Isla. The timing works, and it's the last one for a while. I already told Dad I'm taking off a few months, then coming back part-time after the little man is born. And it's not like I can't bring the baby with me to Crucible." I think my dad actually wants me to bring him with me. I'm not sure who's more excited about this little guy, Mom or Dad.

They've been amazing with Kennedy.

So patient with her, and it paid off in spades. It may have taken her a while to warm up to them, but now they might just be her favorite people in Kroydon Hills. Well, behind Killian, that is. I like to think he's her favorite because he's got the sense of humor of a twelve-year-old boy, making him basically the same age as her. But in all reality, Kennedy is an old soul. She may be more mature than Killian.

It's a topic we've all debated before.

He takes her on ice cream and movie dates whenever she wants.

He bought her love with rocky road.

Not that I didn't buy it with Winnie.

But that's beside the point.

"I guess I just want to keep you safe for as long as I can, Brynn. I'd lock you in the house and bubble-wrap it if I could," he admits, and I know it's those old fears rearing their ugly heads, like they do every now and then. It happens to me too. Every time I feel sick or my body aches in a new or unusual way, I always wonder somewhere deep in the recesses of my soul if maybe the first test was wrong, even though I know it wasn't.

"It's our newest adventure, Deacon. You can't wrap us all in bubble wrap. That's not how our life works," I tell him mid-yawn and snuggle deeper into the blankets.

"Not even just for a few more years?" he asks, and I shake my head no.

"Have you thought anymore about names for the baby?" he asks, and I yawn again,

"I still like Knight," I tell him as my eyes close.

"Knight Kane . . . It does have a nice ring to it."

"Knight Kane sounds like he loves adventures," I whisper as I drift off, faintly aware of my husband's lips against my head. Safe in his arms. Loved. And so happy. I dream about the day I'll meet our son. Our biggest adventure is yet to come.

The End

**Want more Brynlee & Deacon?
Download their extended epilogue!**

Download the extended epilogue here

The Philly Press

KROYDON KRONICLES

NOT READY TO SAY GOODBYE YET?

You didn't think it was over did you?

We still have one more Kroydon Hills socialite who needs her happily ever after.

Make sure to preorder *Tempting*, book 1 in *Red Lips & White Lies*, to see what secrets Kenzie's been keeping…

Preorder Tempting Now

#KroydonKronicles #Tempting

WHAT COMES NEXT?

If you haven't read the first book in the Kings Of Kroydon Hills series, you can start with *All In* today!

Read All In for FREE on KU

ACKNOWLEDGMENTS

This book talks a lot about everything happening for a reason. It may be cliché, but it's something I believe in. It took a lot of things lining up in my life to get me where I am now. And that is something I will be forever grateful for because getting to share this world with all of you has been one of the greatest gifts I've ever been given.

Thank you so much to my family for all of your support. My husband and children are my world and my time with them often gets sacrificed for my time with these characters.

Thank you to my amazing team. I cannot imagine doing this without each and every one of you. Dena, Jen, Tammy, Kelly, Vicki, Morgan, Valentine, Sarah, Shannon and Emma-I have no words big enough to show my appreciation.

And to my incredible momager, Bri. One more series down and an infinite number of books still to go. Thank you for managing my business and my life.

As always, my biggest thanks goes to you, the reader, for taking a chance on Deacon & Brynlee, and this fictional town I love so much. I hope you enjoyed reading The Sweet Spot as much as I've enjoyed writing it.

ABOUT THE AUTHOR

Bella Matthews is a USA Today & Amazon Top 10 Bestselling author. She is married to her very own Alpha Male and raising three little ones. You can typically find her running from one sporting event to another. When she is home, she is usually hiding in her home office with the only other female in her house, her rescue dog Tinker Bell by her side. She likes to write swoon-worthy heroes and sassy, smart heroines. Sarcasm is her love language and big family dynamics are her favorite thing to add to each story.

Stay Connected

Amazon Author Page: https://amzn.to/2UWU7Xs
Facebook Page: https://www.facebook.com/bella.matthews.3511
Reader Group: https://www.facebook.com/groups/599671387345008/
Instagram: https://www.instagram.com/bellamatthews.author/
Bookbub: https://www.bookbub.com/authors/bella-matthews
Goodreads: https://www.goodreads.com/.../show/20795160.Bella_Matthews
TikTok: https://vm.tiktok.com/ZMdfNfbQD/
Newsletter: https://bit.ly/BMNLsingups
Patreon: https://www.patreon.com/BellaMatthews

ALSO BY BELLA MATTHEWS

Kings of Kroydon Hills

All In

More Than A Game

Always Earned, Never Given

Under Pressure

Restless Kings

Rise of the King

Broken King

Fallen King

The Risks We Take Duet

Worth The Risk

Worth The Fight

Defiant Kings

Caged

Shaken

Iced

Overruled

Haven

Playing To Win

The Keeper

The Wildcat

The Knockout

The Sweet Spot

Red Lips & White Lies

Tempting

Redeeming

Enticing

Captivating

Teasing

CHECK OUT BELLA'S WEBSITE

Scan the QR code or go to http://authorbellamatthews.com
to stay up to date with all things Bella Matthews

Printed in Great Britain
by Amazon